ONCE
AND
DONE

ONCE
AND
DONE

JEFF ESHENOUR

TATE PUBLISHING
AND ENTERPRISES, LLC

Published by Tate Publishing & Enterprises, LLC
127 E. Trade Center Terrace | Mustang, Oklahoma 73064 USA
1.888.361.9473 | www.tatepublishing.com

Tate Publishing is committed to excellence in the publishing industry. The company reflects the philosophy established by the founders, based on Psalm 68:11,
"The Lord gave the word and great was the company of those who published it."

Published in the United States of America

ISBN: 978-1-68270-866-8
1. Fiction / Christian / General
2. Fiction / Religious
16.04.22

To my brother Tim
who has shown me more than
anyone that my life is "once and done."
Your perseverance and dedication to the gospel of
Jesus Christ has challenged me more
than you will ever know.

To my parents
who prepared me both
spiritually and academically
for my own college adventure.
Your examples of how to live a godly
life in this day and age mean the world to me.

Acknowledgments

I am so grateful for the people who helped me prepare this book for publishing. A great big thank-you goes out to John Langel for his encouragement and suggestions. John, you share my passion for the written word in a way that very few do. I am deeply indebted to Wayne Loper for spending hours on editing. Wayne, I think it was you who made me believe that I should actually pursue publishing. Thanks also to Patti McCarty who reviewed the manuscript and made many edits. Patti, you caught mistakes that no one else did!

To my grandparents, parents, siblings, and friends who encouraged me during this process, thank you for your uplifting words. To my wife, Brie, thank you for loving and supporting me as I published my first book. I love you so much! Lastly, and most importantly, to Jesus Christ, thank you for loving me in my ugliness, dying in my place, and rising my victorious Savior! May my life be the expression of my thanks.

Contents

Preface

The idea for this book came to me in June 2007. I remember that I was spending time on my knees before God. While praying in my bedroom, the plot came to me in a flash. I believe it was a divine inspiration from God. I had never thought about writing a book before, yet there I was with most of the storyline and even the title. I don't know why God gave this story to me; I wasn't even praying about this subject. But the fact remains that He did, and now I'm giving it to you.

This story is about a young man who falls in love with the most amazing person in the universe. What happens as a result will permanently change his life and the lives of many others. Your life can be just as amazing as his, but only when you realize that it is "once and done."

1

Danger in the Park

Dew-sprinkled grass covered the shady area beneath the towering maple trees in the picnic area of the park. Bees droned lazily from flower to flower, collecting pollen like magnets picking up metal shavings. Clouds played tag from one end of the sky to the other. As the morning sun rose and began warming the earth, a small child of seven years knelt in the sandbox of the playground, happily patting a mound of sand as his mother chatted with a friend at a picnic table twenty feet away.

In this peaceful, pristine setting, a disaster stood ready to strike; alongside the playground stood a tall replica of a Native American totem pole. Hidden inside the pole for years, termites had been slowly eating away its foundation. It had reached critical stage and now the rotting base could no longer support the weight of the pole. Suddenly it began to topple. The mother watched through glazed eyes as it began to fall toward her unprotected child.

As it fell, time seemed to stand still.

"*David!*"

Hearing the scream, the small child instinctively pulled his hands back and sat up to look at his mother. In the next moment, the totem pulverized the mound of sand he was shaping and bounced away from the child, leaving him unscathed.

———⟫●⟪———

Pulling out of his reverie, David Pearl continued jogging down a narrow path in a park very similar to the one in which he had almost lost his life thirteen years ago. It all seemed like a dream to him, even though he could remember quite clearly the huge pole crashing down in front of him. David shuddered and wondered, as he often did, what would have happened if he had been hit by the pole. If it had crushed his hands, both arms would probably have been amputated, and it very easily could have killed him.

What if I had died that day? David asked himself. *Where would my parents be now? And what about me, would I have gone to heaven? I'm not sure I would have.* David was an intellectual; he loved to think. The what-ifs from his past seemed to nip at his heels as he ran the familiar path.

David emerged from the woods and continued jogging toward the parking lot and around an area where workers were erecting a monstrous wooden tower to be used for rappelling training. The area was surrounded by a chain link fence and

David ran past, as he had every other morning, without a second glance. Construction seemed to be proceeding slowly on the tower. Absorbed in his thoughts, he saw nothing until a loud shout alerted him to danger. As he turned, a gigantic construction log came hurtling out of the sky. It smashed into the top of the chain link fence, crumpling it like an accordion. Without time to react, David was battered to the ground as one end of the log bounced into his legs, hurling him headfirst into a rock. Everything went black.

———>•<———

"Mr. and Mrs. Pearl? The doctor would like to see you now." David's parents followed the nurse halfway down a corridor and into the doctor's office. They had received a phone call from the hospital about David's accident and had driven the two hours to Pinevale knowing only that David had been in some type of accident.

Doctor Mallory was a short man who by habit spoke hesitantly in a rather nasally voice, which didn't help to put the couple at ease. "Mr. and Mrs. ah, Pearl, I, er, presume?"

They nodded and Mr. Pearl asked impatiently, "How is David? Is he going to be all right?"

Doctor Mallory nodded. "By all our tests and x-rays, er, the boy is doing, ahem, amazingly well."

Mr. and Mrs. Pearl sighed in relief. Mrs. Pearl spoke up, "We were so worried because we couldn't get any details over the phone."

The doctor cleared his throat. "Ahem, mm, yes and so you should have been, er, ma'am. You know, the boy is really, ah, lucky to still be swimming in the pond with the other fish if you, hmm, er, know what I mean." Doctor Mallory was not very tactful.

The nurse piped up, "Your son really is lucky. If that log had hit him anywhere in the upper body, it could have done so much damage that we might have had trouble stopping the internal bleeding. It could have even killed him outright. As it is, however, the log only hit his legs. His left leg is broken in one spot, but if he stays off it for a while, it should heal quickly. His other leg has a nasty scrape, but other than that nothing is wrong…except for the rather large bump where he hit his head."

"Yes, er, here are the x-rays," said Doctor Mallory. "As you can see there is only, er, really one point of damage and that is, hm, here." He stopped and pointed with his pen. "Right between the, mm, knee and the ankle. This is a, ah, rather serious break, but like any other fracture it should, uh, heal all right. Mm, we already have it, er, in a, ahem, cast."

"Right," said Mrs. Pearl. "Can we go see him now? I've been waiting for so long, and I just want to see him and make sure that he's fine."

"Sure," the nurse said, smiling. "Follow me and I'll take you to his room."

David Pearl lay back on his hospital bed, stretched, and let out a huge hippopotamus yawn. Thankfully, the pain he was experiencing now was only a dull throb due to all the medications he had been given. He was still a bit groggy, but he had had plenty of time to ponder his close call as he lay there with his leg in a cast. He knew he was lucky to be alive.

That log was huge. It could've snuffed out my life like a candle. For the second time that day, he found himself wondering what would have happened if he had died, but he knew that this time he would have gone to heaven. His thoughts turned back to that day when he was ten years old and his life took a turn for the better. David's mother had prayed for years that her husband would come to Christ. He remembered quite clearly how his dad had asked Jesus to be the Lord of his life and how it had changed everything about him. His dad no longer cursed and swore at his mom, and David didn't have to worry about becoming the object of his father's wrath if he did something wrong. His dad had been completely changed, and David knew that he wanted that change too. He remembered sitting on the couch with his mom a few months later as he prayed and asked Jesus to take control of his life, forgive him for his mistakes, and make him a new person. Ever since that moment, David knew he would go to heaven when he died.

But this close call made him think hard about dying. *Would I really have been ready to die? Did I accomplish all the things I should have up to this point? Did I truly live a worthwhile life?*

It had been an exhausting day, and slowly David's thoughts melted away as he fell into a deep sleep.

———⟫●⟪———

As Mr. and Mrs. Pearl stepped quietly into the room, the nurse nodded to them and withdrew. They walked to his bed and stood silently, studying their only child. David was of average build with broad shoulders and an even broader smile. He was usually a very jolly fellow with a hearty laugh that he used easily and frequently. His chestnut brown hair was trimmed into a crew cut, and he had large brown eyes that possessed a wide range of emotions. Mr. and Mrs. Pearl had noticed on several occasions that David's eyes seemed to take on a life of their own, appearing deep and mysterious. David was athletic but did fairly well with his studies too. They didn't come easy to him, but he studied hard and received good grades.

The Pearls stood looking proudly at their son, tears welling in their eyes as they realized how blessed they were that although the accident had the potential to be serious, his injuries were minor and they still had him with them. They each gave a quick prayer of thanks to God for keeping His hand of protection on their son. Mrs. Pearl finally moved to the side of the bed and rubbed the back of David's hand. His eyelids fluttered as he awoke and tried to focus. Seeing his parents, his teeth flashed in a sleepy grin and he announced, "'Bout time you got here! I got so tired of waiting I took a nap!"

Mr. Pearl patted him on the back. "Good to see you all in one piece, son!"

"What happened?" asked Mrs. Pearl. "We couldn't seem to get the full scoop from anybody."

David reached for the control panel and raised his bed to get more comfortable. "I was running in Arrow Springs State Park. That's the one just three blocks from Pinevale University. I can easily get there from the campus, and it has a nice flat terrain for jogging."

David's father interrupted. "We assumed that, but all we could learn about the accident was that somehow a support beam for that rappelling tower fell and banged you up. We can't understand how it cleared the fence if it dropped from the tower. That tower is a good thirty feet inside the fence!"

"Yeah, I was a little confused about that too," David admitted. "But the doctor told me the beam didn't fall off the tower, it fell as the crane was hoisting it. Apparently, the chain around it wasn't secure, and it slipped out as it was being raised. The way the crane was sitting, the arm has to swing out close to the fence to reach the tower. That's why the log bounced and was able to hit me. I'm one lucky boy."

"Yes, you are," agreed his father. "We're so thankful the Lord was watching over you. How do you feel now?"

"Well, I guess okay, considering what happened. Right now my leg doesn't hurt too badly, but my head's throbbing a little, and I have a nice goose egg where I hit that rock." David chuckled. "You should see the rock though. Split in two!"

2

FRESNETT AND HUTCHENS

Two days later, David sat in his wheelchair, looking out the sliding glass doors onto the patio of the Pearls' country house. David was in his third year of college at Pinevale University. Pinevale was a mid-sized, semi-countrified town located about two hours north of David's home. It was spring break, and interestingly enough the accident had happened on Saturday, the very first day of break. David was supposed to have left for home later that day but decided that he would go for his usual morning run in the park before leaving. *I can be glad this didn't happen in the middle of classes,* thought David. He wondered how different it would be going to classes in a wheelchair or crutches when he went back to school. He wasn't looking forward to it, but he knew he could handle it.

———✦———

Bzzz! Bzzz! David's phone began vibrating in his pocket. He'd been getting a boatload of calls as word began to get out about his accident. He struggled to pull the phone out of his front pocket and saw a number he didn't recognize on the screen. He answered anyway, "Hello, this is David."

"Ya'r once 'n' dun," came a garbled voice from the other end. There was a little bit of static on the line.

"Excuse me?" David still had no idea who it was, and he couldn't imagine what "once and done" was supposed to mean. At least that's what it had sounded like.

The voice spoke again, emphasizing each syllable. "You…are…a…*dunce*…to…run!"

David laughed. There was no question now who it was. Donald Fresnett was his roommate at college as well as his best friend. Donald did not enjoy running, and the ongoing joke was that David would someday get Donald to go running with him. Donald adamantly refused and was always telling David he was insane to get up so early in the morning to keep himself from getting eaten by wood flies.

"And why is that, Mr. Fresnett?"

"Isn't it quite obvious, there, Sir Pearl? If you wouldn't insist on running all the time, this wouldn't have happened! Now you see why I don't run with you!"

David couldn't resist. "Well, I'm sure if you had been there, nothing would have happened to me."

"Oh yeah? Why's that?"

"Well, I would have been a lot further behind, always listening to you complaining, and I would have had to run a lot slower so you could keep up! That log would have already been off the path by the time we got there!"

"Oh, haha. Very funny." There was a slight pause and David heard Donald laughing.

"By the way, Donny, why aren't you calling from your cell phone? I don't recognize this number."

"This is my house phone. I don't get good reception when I'm at home. But how are you feeling anyway?"

"Well, not too bad, aside from having a busted shinbone, my whole leg in a cast, and a knot on my head the size of a softball! Not too bad!"

"Oh, stop your whining, Dave. Give it to me straight. How's it feel to have your leg encased in a piece of concrete?"

"Well, it's not exactly concrete, Donald, but sometimes it feels just as heavy." David raised his leg which caused some discomfort. "Thankfully, I don't have too much pain. I've been confined to a wheelchair and it'll be about two weeks 'til I can get around on crutches. School should be quite interesting."

Now it was Donald's turn to give David another jab. "At least this will stop you from running all the time."

David just laughed. "You're just jealous, Donny, that's all. You're jealous of my bagpipe lungs and steel calf muscles."

"No, I'm not," answered Donald sarcastically. "I'm jealous of all the welts you get from being bitten by all those wood flies. Those things are like killer bees!"

"Okay, whatever you say, Donny. Hey, pray for me, will ya? This could really tie me down with schoolwork and other activities. I don't need this right now. Pray that I can recover quickly because I can't imagine the nuisance it's going to be trying to get around campus with a broken leg."

"Sure, man. I'll storm the throne room of heaven for you. God's going to get so sick of hearing me asking for your healing that He's gonna do it just to get rid of me!"

"Okay, sounds great, Donny!"

"I'll see you later, man."

"Yup…bye."

———⫸●⫷———

Andrea Hutchens was singing quietly to herself as she tidied up her room. She couldn't imagine where she had put her slippers. *How can something that I use so often get lost so easily? Oh well, at least my room will be spic and span by the time I'm done.* She smiled to herself. Oh, how easy it was to make a messy room. Glancing around her sanctum, she saw the numerous pictures on her walls. She had only been on break for three days, but she already missed her friends. Especially him. *I wonder…*

The muffled sound of her ringing cell phone caught her attention. "Now where in the world is my cell phone?" she asked aloud. She finally located the sound coming from beneath a book on her window seat. "There it is!" Andrea laughed out loud when she saw the phone tucked neatly into one of her slippers beneath the book. Still giggling, she answered the phone. "Hello?"

"Hey, Andrea, what are you up to?"

"David Pearl! Oh, not much. This and that, you know. By the way, thank you."

"Thank you? For what?"

"For finding my slippers for me!" She burst out laughing.

"What in the world are you talking about?"

Andrea explained and then asked, "So what's new with you? Are you staying occupied over break?"

"Which break? Spring break or the break in my leg? What's new, you ask? Not much, other than I'm now living in a wheelchair." David wasn't sure what kind of reaction this would get.

"*What?* What happened?"

David proceeded to explain the accident, which elicited gasps from Andrea. He concluded by saying, "So I just need you to pray for me, okay? I'm not looking forward to school in this condition."

"Absolutely, Dave. I just wish I could see you."

He smiled at the sincerity in her voice. "Seeing me wouldn't fix my leg, you know."

"I know, but I would feel better being able to see you in person."

"Whatever. Hey, there's an evangelist with a healing ministry coming to our Wednesday night church service tomorrow night. I don't want to get my hopes up too much, but it would be awesome if God healed me outright. Pray that His will would be done."

"Sure. I'll do that, Dave. Thanks for calling and letting me know."

"No problem. Thanks for everything."

"Yup. I'll see ya."

"Okay, bye."

Andrea hung up and closed her eyes, not wanting to believe what she had just heard. She was quite thankful that nothing worse had happened. She very easily could've lost him and she never wanted that to happen. *Yes you will see me all right. And sooner than you expected.*

3

Fire

It had been a long time since David's church had heard the type of preaching it was receiving now. The evangelist, Andrew Blake, was someone who told it like it was. He didn't mince words or preach in order to tickle people's ears. Pastor Blake was determined to speak straight from the heart of God regardless of the response. He knew that only when he let God take charge would the Lord move in the hearts and lives of those who were ready. Now he was in the middle of his sermon and things were starting to heat up.

"The Lord says in Revelation that He wants us to be either hot or cold, not lukewarm. If we are lukewarm, then Jesus tells us that He will spit us out of His mouth! In other words, He will throw us away because we are useless to Him! Today there are too many Christians who are lukewarm—especially here in America. We aren't persecuted, so we don't have to rely on God. We end up relying on ourselves, and how many of you know that when we rely on ourselves, things go wrong? Proverbs 14:12 says, 'There is a way which seems right to a man, but its end is the way of death.'" There were some nods of agreement, but many people began to squirm in their seats, forced to consider what was an uncomfortable truth. But Pastor Blake was just getting started.

"I don't need to describe who the lukewarm people are. You know if you're lukewarm. You know if you're not so hungry for God that you make it your first priority to spend time with Him each day! You know if you are not so burdened over the lost souls going to hell that you can't help but share the gospel with those around you! You know if you are not so sold out to God that you don't *care* what happens to you! Yes, you know if you're lukewarm. We are not called to be lukewarm. We are called to be hot or cold. Let's talk about being hot." David's wheelchair was in the front row of the sanctuary, and he began getting hot himself. Something inside of him had just clicked, but he did not know what it was.

"Let me talk about fire for a little," Pastor Blake continued. "God's fire is what we need in our lives. The fire of God is what enables us to reach out to people, speak truth into their lives, and lead them to Christ. Without the fire of God in our lives, we will never get anywhere. I like to compare this to the old railroad trains that used to burn coal. Those trains would never move unless there was a fire burning inside them. The bigger the fire, the faster it would go. And the fire would always be there inside the engine, providing the power for it to go. As soon as the fire died down the train would stop. We are just like that train. Peter, Paul, and all the other disciples and apostles in the Bible had a burning passion inside of them that pushed them onward. That's why they didn't care if they were whipped, beaten, starved, thrown in prison, or killed. They only wanted to live for Jesus. They knew that what mattered was not what happened to them in this life, but what happened in eternity. They had the fire of God. They were hot!

"But let me tell you something." Pastor Blake paused to wipe the sweat from his brow with a handkerchief. He was not a preacher who liked to stand still. Instead he would pace the platform, often gesturing to emphasize certain points. "It's uncomfortable to get burned with fire." He paused. "You see, fire hurts, and it also hurts for the Christian who desires the fire of God. Do you know why? Because for God to really work through you, He has to be in complete control of your life! He cannot be impeded by anything! You cannot have other idols in your life! You can't hold on to secret sins in your life! If you are a captive to alcohol, cutting, pornography, or drugs, God won't have freedom to move in your life! If you watch TV, play sports, and relax more than you pray and read your Bible, you'll be quenching the Spirit of God! This is why it hurts to get the fire of God! Because in order for Him to use you, He has to burn the impurities away until you are clean and empty of everything else so that He has control. Your life has to be all about Him! You must put Him first in every aspect of your life! Every word you say, every action you do, every friend you have, every thought you think, every relationship you build, and every place you go must be about Him! God must have first place!

"We are going to bring this message to a close. God is working in lives, and He wants to change you. He wants to change you—but you have to surrender first. You have to give him your life. I will be down front if you would like me to pray for you. Come for prayer if you have any need, be it physical, emotional, financial, or spiritual. But do not shut God out. If He is speaking to you, do not push Him away. Run to Him. Run to Him.

<hr>

David felt as if he were about to burst. He knew the sermon had been for him. Yeah, he tried to live for Christ, but he knew that he had not given everything over to God. He knew he was still holding tightly to things in his life that should not be there. As soon as Pastor Blake finished his last word, David pushed himself forward until he was right in front of the pulpit. Andrew Blake was not even off the platform when he saw David waiting. He smiled. He was not surprised in the least that this young boy in a wheelchair had come forward for prayer.

As Pastor Blake approached, David raised his voice to be heard over the worship team which had started to sing. "Pastor, God spoke to me while you were preaching. I need a touch from God. I can feel something is about to happen, I just don't know what. Obviously, I need prayer for my leg, but I also want the fire of God in my life. I want Him to use me to reach others, and He needs to have complete control before that can happen."

Pastor Andrew nodded understandingly. "I can see your desire to give God your life. God wants to fill you with boldness and power, and He will do it if you just surrender completely." He paused to see David's nod of understanding. "What is your name?"

"David."

"Okay, David. Let's pray." Pastor Andrew placed one hand on David's forehead and one on his cast where the leg was broken. After that, David remembered almost nothing. Pastor Blake's prayer was not wordy; rather, it was short and to the point. But David hardly heard any of it. As soon as he felt Andrew Blake's hand on his head, something snapped within David. His body felt like it was burning up on the inside, yet he had goose bumps all up and down his arms and legs. David was not one to cry easily, but tears began streaming down his face, and he did not understand why. All he knew was that he was in the presence of God Almighty and that his life was full of sin that was disgusting in the sight of a holy God.

David just barely caught Pastor Blake's closing words. "Lord, I thank you for this life that is broken and hungry for more of You. Make Yourself real to him, Father. And we pray this in the name of Jesus. Amen." He bent down close and whispered in David's ear, "I know you want to live completely for the Lord. Let me challenge you to never lose sight of that desire. Expend your life for Jesus in whatever ways He asks. You only have one chance. Make sure you get it accomplished while you can because your life is once and done!"

———>●<———

David lost all concept of time. He sat at the front of the church in his wheelchair, soaking in the presence of God. Never had the Lord's touch been so real. Never had he felt such peace in his life. He did not want it to end. His whole being was focused on God. The people around him, the congregation, the singing, all ceased to exist around him; he heard nothing else and saw nothing else. All he could do was sit and worship.

Pastor Blake had moved on to pray for other people, and the congregation began to disperse. Still, David sat unmoving, oblivious to all that was going on around him. Suddenly, he felt two hands rest softly on his shoulders and heard someone praying quietly. He didn't even bother looking up; he just wanted this moment to go on forever. Finally, he raised his head, realizing for the first time that even the worship team was coming down from the platform. He turned in his seat to see who was behind him, and as he looked up he almost fell out of the wheelchair. Standing behind him was none other than Andrea Hutchens!

———◆———

Andrea almost laughed out loud at the look of undisguised shock on David's face. Instead, she held a finger to her lips and pointed to the side of the room. Dumbfounded, David nodded and wheeled himself over to the pews. He looked at Andrea again as if skeptical at what his own eyes were telling him. She was a thin girl of average height and flowing golden-brown hair that dropped below her shoulders. Her thin brows were quick to bounce up and down with emotion or bunch up in thought. Andrea loved to laugh, and when she did, her perfect teeth sparkled with joy.

She sat down beside David on the pew and spoke in a quiet tone so as not to disturb the few people still praying in the mostly dark sanctuary. "Surprised to see me?" she asked with a chuckle.

"I don't think 'surprised' is the right word," replied David. "Try *stunned*."

Andrea smiled. "I just had to see you after we talked yesterday."

"Well, now that you've seen me, do you approve?"

"No. You're not supposed to go around breaking your legs, Dave. What if something worse had happened and I had lost you?"

"You'd do the same thing all my other family and friends would have done—mourned for a while but gone on living your life. But that's not the point. I didn't die. Someday I will though, so don't upset yourself too much when it happens. Just remember that when it happens, I'm at home with my Savior! Anyhow, God protected me and here I am, but how did you get here?"

"Well, I decided after our phone call that I was going to try to make it to this service tonight. Nothing else was on my schedule so I got my things together and drove here. I arrived a bit late, which is why I didn't talk to you beforehand. When I saw you staying up front for so long, I figured I'd come up and pray for you a little."

"Thanks. Every little bit helps. Are you driving back tonight? That's going to make a late night for you."

"Nope. I'm spending the night. You know that sweet little white-haired lady that comes to this church, Lois Reed? I stayed with her once before when I came here for those revival services. I called her up, and she agreed to let me stay again. Such a darling! Oh! And I'm also taking you home. When you stayed at the altar for so long, I told your parents that I would get you home."

David looked around and noticed with some surprise that his parents were gone. In fact, they were practically the only ones left in the sanctuary. He looked for Pastor Blake but couldn't find him anywhere. "Well, I guess we better head home then. Let's go."

⟶⟫●⟪⟵

David wheeled himself across the parking lot with Andrea keeping pace beside him. The stars shone brightly through the cloudless night. David's sense of euphoria still hung with him. He had never experienced the joy and peace that was filling him now. When they got to the car, he slowly stood up on his good leg, took two short hops, and lowered himself backward into the front seat of the car. Wryly, he commented, "Sorry, but you're going to have to pick that wheelchair up by yourself."

"Don't apologize. I can handle it. Just tell me how to fold the thing up."

With some confusion on Andrea's part and many laughs together, she finally managed to get it closed up. Andrea lifted it slowly and shoved it into the backseat before going around to the driver's side. David smiled at her and said, "Thanks, Andi."

"No problem!" Her teeth flashed in the moonlight.

Andrea started the car and moved out of the parking lot onto the street. The next few minutes passed in silence. The roads were deserted, and all was quiet except for the soft purring of the motor. As they eased out of the town and into the country, the stars became even more pronounced. A raccoon ambled off into the bushes beside the road.

"I'm changed, Andrea." David's tone of voice was so assertive and packed with meaning that Andrea looked over at him sharply before returning her eyes to the road. His elbow was positioned on the armrest, and his chin was cradled on his palm as he stared straight out the windshield.

"What do you mean?" she asked.

"Back there, at the church…" his voice trailed off. He was having problems putting his feelings into words.

"Yes…" Andrea probed.

"I've never experienced what I did tonight. The Lord changed my life in a way that I just can't seem to explain. I know I'm not the same. I was a Christian before, but I wasn't really living the life that I was supposed to." Andrea felt a chill run up her spine and goose bumps spread down her arm. David continued, "From here on out, I'm going to start *living* for Jesus. And I mean *everything* is to be about Him. Not that I won't mess up. It's going to be a process. But from here on out, I do what He says no matter what that may be. I go where He wants me to go, and I say what He wants me to say. Pastor Blake prayed for me and gave me a sort of challenge. He told me to expend my life for the purposes of God. I can quote his last sentences word for word. He said, 'You only have one chance. Make sure you get it accomplished while you can because your life is once and done!' Those last six words hit me hard. *Really* hard. My life is once and done! This is it! Now I see why God kept me alive in that accident. He wasn't quite done with me, and He used this service tonight to show me that I need to get with the program or I'm going to waste my life chasing after meaningless things!" He paused. "I'm sorry...I didn't mean to go on like that."

Andrea hesitated a moment before answering, "It's all right." She had been somewhat taken aback by his outburst. As she had listened, she could barely believe the emotion in his words. She had never heard David or anyone else speak the way he just had. It was said with such a quiet vehemence that she never doubted one word of his declaration. Andrea had been hoping that God would heal David's leg at this service, and to be perfectly honest with herself, she probably would prefer to have him physically restored rather than spiritually renewed. However, she knew that God was in control and that He knew best. She wished she had reached that spot in her walk with God where David now was, but she knew she had not yet obtained that kind of zeal. Andrea was also a little dubious about what would happen next. It was obvious that something had tugged at David's heart, and she was sure there would be changes in his life, but she just wasn't sure if she would like the consequences.

———⊷●⊶———

David got in bed that night with a sigh. It was a pain sleeping with a cast, but tonight he didn't mind at all. His thoughts were all about the events of the evening. He felt so happy, and he wanted it to last forever. He thought about his conversation with Andrea. He was not quite sure what she had thought when he had shared his emotions with her. Andrea was a Christian and was seeking after God herself, but David didn't know how she had taken his outburst. His thoughts turned to their relationship. He guessed that he was in love with her. They had been friends since their first semester at Pinevale University, and over the last year David found himself being attracted to her more and more. He assumed she felt the same way, but nothing had ever been said about it. However, tonight, with the presence of God still strong in his spiritual senses, David knew that he couldn't let his relationship with Andrea get between himself and God. She could not be a distraction in his relationship with the Lord. He knew that he had to put Jesus first in every area of his life and that meant drawing closer to God than to Andrea. "Man, that is so hard," he whispered to himself in the darkness. "But it is because I love her that I must wait. It is because I love her that I must draw closer to Christ now. I'm going to go after God with everything I've got while keeping a good, pure friendship with Andrea. If she catches fire and runs with me, great. If she doesn't, well, God is in control and He is all that matters right now."

Andrea pulled slowly up the driveway to Lois Reed's house. After turning off the engine, she sat silently for a moment in the dark, trying to collect her thoughts. Finally she got out of the car and walked to the side of the house where she slowly mounted the stairs to the deck. The door was unlocked as Mrs. Reed had said it would be, and Andrea entered quietly. The light was on above the kitchen table, and Andrea saw a note waiting for her.

> *Dear Andrea,*
>
> *I'm delighted you are staying the night. Please make yourself at home. I didn't know how late you would be so I didn't stay up for you. There are milk and cookies in the fridge that I baked this afternoon. Help yourself. We'll talk in the morning. Good night!*
>
> *Mrs. Reed*

Andrea smiled. What a dear lady! Mrs. Reed had always been a saint. Andrea had a quick snack before climbing the stairs to the guest bedroom. She was familiar with the house from her previous visit. She dropped her duffel bag onto a chair and flopped down on the big bouncy bed. Exhausted from the evening, she knew if she lay there too long she would fall asleep, so she forced herself to get up and begin getting ready for bed. After switching off the bedside light, she slid in under the heavy covers and snuggled down with a deep sigh.

But sleep did not come easy to Andrea. She could not get David's words out of her head. She remembered sitting and talking in the car after they had arrived at David's house. She had looked over at David and he was staring straight at her as he talked. His eyes were still vivid in her mind as she lay there, attempting without success to fall asleep. Those eyes. They were soft with emotion yet rock hard with determination. At times David's eyes seemed to have a life of their own. Andrea knew David was not the same. She knew it was a good thing because she knew that God had really touched him, but somehow she was not as happy as she thought she should be. *Maybe I'm a little jealous. Maybe he won't care about me as much now that he's really living for Jesus.* Andrea tossed and turned in the spacious bed, and her thoughts were just as restless. *Maybe I'm a little convicted because I'm not living that kind of dedicated life. I don't know. I just don't know!* Andrea whispered the last sentence aloud as she voiced her frustration. "Oh God, I don't want things to change! I love David! I love You too, and I want to live for You, but I don't want David to forget about me in his zeal for You. I'm sorry, Lord, that I have this attitude. Please help me work this all out! I need You, Jesus."

The eastern sky blazed in radiant glory as the sun peeked over the hills and began its slow ascent into the heavens. Rays of golden light bounced off the pond and reflected into David's eyes through the bedroom window. Slowly he rolled over and opened his eyes. A new day, a new beginning. David let last evening's events roll around in his mind. He smiled. He felt so clean and light inside. This is what life was all about: living with purpose! Today he began his new life as a servant of the Lord. He was living for Jesus!

———◆———

The same sun warmed the earth four miles away. A squirrel scampered up the big maple tree, sat down, twitched, and began scolding a beetle that had tickled his tail as it ambled by. A bird twittered. Andrea yawned and stretched. She lay in bed for several minutes without moving. She smiled. Last night, as she was crying out to God, she actually began to feel a peace about the whole situation. This morning she felt invigorated and ready to face life again. She had determined that she would follow David's lead. She knew she did not yet have the drive and determination that he had, but she hoped she would achieve it soon. For now she had decided to join David in following the Lord. She didn't really know what this would require, but she wanted to try even though she knew it would be hard. Andrea felt like she had a new purpose in life. Today, as the Lord began to lead, she would be following. She was living for Jesus!

4

A New Week

It was Sunday afternoon and Mr. and Mrs. Pearl were driving David back to Pinevale for his first week of classes after spring break. He was ready to come back to college with the joy of the Lord in his heart. In fact, ever since last Sunday evening's service, David was not that worried about being in a wheelchair for his classes. He was ready to come back to school bringing the new joy that he was experiencing with him.

Pulling through the main gate of the college, the familiar sight of the Welcome Fountain in front of the flagpole came into view. So named because it was the first thing a person saw as they entered the campus, the Welcome Fountain had become synonymous with Pinevale University and appeared on many of the college publications.

As they drove through the campus, David began recognizing fellow students walking on the sidewalk and throwing Frisbees on the college lawn. "Oh, the blessings we take for granted," David mused out loud. "I bet those guys never thought about what it would be like to be unable to run around in a field throwing a Frisbee."

"That is very true," commented Mr. Pearl. "But you probably didn't either until you busted up your leg," he said with a grin.

"Yeah, you're probably right."

They drove on in silence for a little while. As they neared the on-campus housing complex where David's room was located, he spoke again, "God has given me such a burden for this college. Ever since my accident, He's really shown me that He has a plan for me on this campus. I can't wait to see what He does."

Mrs. Pearl spoke up, "That's exciting, son. We'll definitely be praying for you. Keep your ears attentive to what the Holy Spirit says to you. I can't wait to hear what happens."

<hr>

Moving back into his room was different for David this time. In fact, he didn't do anything. He couldn't. He felt like he was just getting in the way. He was thankful that his room was on the first floor so that they didn't have to bother with the elevator all the time. Pushing himself over to the bed, he gave his parents instructions on where to put his belongings. There weren't many things since he had only been gone for a week, and soon it was done.

David looked at his watch. "I wonder where Donny is," he mused. "I would've guessed that he'd be around at this time of day." No sooner were the words out of his mouth than a smiling face popped around the corner of the open door followed by the small frame of Donald Fresnett.

"You guessed right! I'm right here, roomie! How are you doing?"

"None the better for having seen your ugly mug! You have that mischievous look on your face. What have you been up to, you rascal?"

Donny walked over and plopped down on his bed without the least bit of concern over David's jibe. "Ugly mug yourself, bootbrain. What did you do? Put your face in the blender over spring break? You must shatter the mirror each time you look into it!"

"Oh yeah? Well, you…"

"Now boys," interrupted David's mother, "that's quite enough of that!"

"It's okay, Mom." David grinned. "This is the only language Donny knows. If someone didn't throw friendly insults at him, he'd have no conversation at all! You don't have to worry, we wouldn't think of doing this kind of thing with anyone else. This is how we lighten things up—by having friendly word wars."

"Just don't let it get out of hand," said Mrs. Pearl.

"Oh, it never gets out of hand does it, dwarfbrain?" David smiled slyly at Donny.

"Nope! Never…" Donny's voice trailed off momentarily before he retorted. "Lardbelly!"

Mrs. Pearl sighed and shook her head. Instantly, Donny shot up off the bed and with exaggerated elegance bowed to Mrs. Pearl, transforming into the perfect gentleman. Mimicking a British accent he said, "Surely, Ma'am, you don't think we truly mean such verbal atrocities, do you? If it has bothered you, I would sooner go sit on a rock for three days than to hurt your precious feelings again. Will you accept my humblest apologies, Your Ladyness?"

Pure innocence and regret was plastered all over Donald's face, and Mrs. Pearl couldn't help but burst out laughing. "All right, you little beguiler! Quit your flattering. Besides, 'Ladyness' is not a word."

Donny's pretense disappeared in an instant as he turned to David. "She sounds just like you, always correcting my English." He changed his voice in an attempt to mimic David, "It's *more fun,* Donny, not *funner.* It's 'John and *I,*' not 'John and *me.*'" In a normal voice he continued, "Look, I know I'm back at college, but technically I'm still on break, so don't be bothering me about school-related stuff. School doesn't start until tomorrow."

David just laughed.

He was cut short by a whole bunch of people piling into the room. A female voice said, "Well, it's good to see you can still laugh with your leg in a cast!"

David recognized Andrea's voice and saw that there were at least six other people with her. They were all friends of his from Dunamis, a Christian group on campus. Everyone began talking at once until David held up his hand to quiet them down. "Whoa, whoa! Slow down a bit everyone! One at a time! You first, Derek."

Derek, the student president of Dunamis, asked, "How are you doing, David? Can you tell us exactly what happened?"

David patiently told the story again and ended by saying, "I'm doing pretty well right now. I can't complain. I mean, a few more inches and I could've been killed. I should only have about two more weeks before I can exchange this wheelchair for crutches, which will make it a lot easier to get to classes."

Rebecca, a sophomore at Pinevale, spoke up, "We were all so worried when we heard the news. At first I couldn't believe it had happened!"

David raised one eyebrow as he was prone to do when he was curious. "That reminds me. How *did* all of you know about it? And how did you all know to show up together? How did you know I had arrived?"

Everyone began grinning and John spoke up, "Oh, a little bird told us."

"A little bird, huh? Let me guess. A little Fresnett bird by the name of Donald?" David rounded on his roommate. "Is that why you weren't here when we arrived? You little sneak! You saw us pulling in and went to alert everybody!"

Donny's smile melted David's pretend scowl as he said, "You're just too good, Dave. You're just too good. But aren't you glad I did?"

It was 3:00 in the afternoon on the following day, and David was already sick of being in his wheelchair. He was tired of the cumbersome contraption always getting in the way, and he was tired of getting to classes late. His professors understood because he had notified them previously, but it was still annoying.

Lunch was a huge hassle too. He always had to ask for help in getting the items he wanted, and then it became a balancing act as he pushed himself to the checkout with the tray supported on his lap. He was also tired of everybody asking what had happened. David understood that the inquiries were made with good intentions, but it became monotonous giving an abbreviated version of the story twenty-five times a day.

David's last class had just ended, and he pushed himself toward his housing complex. Thoughts ran through his mind about facing a whole week of this hassle. It frustrated him immensely. Here he was, moping around on his first day back to school after telling himself and everyone else that he was excited about bringing Jesus with him back to campus. *How can I be so wishy-washy?* thought David. *I'm such a weakling! I get all fired up about how Jesus is going to be my number one and how I'm going to live for Him, and then as soon as I hit a little adversity, I crumble! I guess I have a choice to make. How am I going to respond to this hardship? Will I give in and let it conquer me, or will I stand up and make a willful choice to rise above it and be joyful, even in suffering? I knew ever since I rededicated my life to God that it wouldn't be easy and that I would need to press into Him to get through my problems, so I guess now we get to see if I really believe that.*

<hr />

David had resolved to make the best of the situation, but he was still frowning slightly when he wheeled himself into his bedroom. Donny was sitting at his desk when David came in, but popped up and said, "Hey Mr. Sourchops, you look about as happy as a donkey chewing on a green briar! C'mon! Let's go! I've been waiting for you."

"Where are we going?"

"Down to the Lodge…I'm hungry!" The Pinevale Lodge was a central building on campus that served as the student center. Not only did it house several general education classrooms, but it also held the fitness center, convenience store, game room, TV lounge, a dining facility, and a larger room for activities such as school dances and talent shows. This large room, called the Rendezvous, was where Dunamis met for their weekly meetings.

David was getting a little hungry himself and didn't protest when Donny insisted on pushing him to the dining facility in the Lodge, appropriately named The Kitchen. Donny wheeled him out of the room and down the hall to exit the dorm. When they reached the sidewalk, Donny suddenly took off and charged headlong across campus.

David grabbed the side handles of the wheelchair to steady himself. "Whoa! Slow it down there a bit, Donald!"

Donny pretended not to hear and, laughing, sprinted down the walk. Students skittered out of the way as Donny charged past yelling, "Gangway! Beep beep! Comin' through!" Bystanders began laughing as David kept yelling at his friend, "Holy smoke, Donald! Slow down, you're going to wreck us! Stop!"

Directly in front of the Lodge, the sidewalk turned to the right before reaching the entrance. David braced himself as Donny lunged into the curve at full speed while trying to make the turn. He was going too fast, however, and the turn was just a *little too* sharp. Donny tried to slow down, but it was too late! Overshooting the bend, the wheelchair shot off the sidewalk.

Crunch! David's legs disappeared into the soft-branched bushes that constituted a hedge in front of the Lodge. "Oh shoot, David! Are you all right?" Donny asked apprehensively. "Your leg isn't hurt, is it?"

Grimacing, David scowled at his roommate. "I don't think so, but that's with no thanks to you!" Seeing Donny's face droop, David began laughing out loud. "I betcha we were quite a sight racing down the sidewalk! What got into you anyway?"

Donny brightened up a bit. "I don't know. I guess I just saw your long face when you came into our room and decided you needed some excitement. I'm glad you're not hurt."

"Yeah, me too," replied David. "Just don't do that again, okay? And hey! Why in the world won't you run like that with me when I'm *not* in the wheelchair?"

Donny laughed. "Probably because when you're in the wheelchair, *I* get to pick the speed!"

Donald pushed David up the ramp and through the double doors into the lobby of the Lodge. As they proceeded down the hall, David began to smell the aroma of dinner wafting from The Kitchen. *That's the problem*, he thought wryly, *college food always smells better than it tastes.*

Like many times before, David immediately became aware of the cozy atmosphere as he entered The Kitchen. The room was designed to resemble the inside of a rustic log structure. In one corner was a fireplace that blazed brightly in the winter. Other lighting was subdued except along the side where the buffet counters stood. At The Kitchen, you could pay a set price and have an all-you-can-eat meal. This was one of David's favorite dining facilities on campus. Students not only came here to eat, but often just hung out in the comfy stuffed furniture along the far edge of the room and by the fireplace.

Before the two roommates could get very far into the room, an electric wheelchair came buzzing around one of the tables and zipped past them out into the hall. It was moving at a fast clip, but David managed to get a look at the face of the student who occupied it. He just managed to turn in time to see the wheelchair disappear around the corner. The boy's head was down as if he was ashamed to be seen, but from David's lower view, he could see that there was a tear running down the student's face.

"I wonder who that was," David mused aloud.

"I don't know, but I've seen him around before," replied Donny.

"Yeah, I've seen him before too. But did you see his face?"

"No. What about it?"

"He was crying. Something was wrong."

"I'm sure he's fine. He probably just had a long day."

"Yeah, I know what that's like." But David was still wondering about the student in the wheelchair. His mind pondered the endless possibilities of what could have been making him cry.

"Hey look!" Donny's exclamation pulled David back to reality as he pointed toward the corner. "There are some of the fellows and fellowettes from Dunamis!"

David laughed. "Fellowettes?"

"Yeah! Female fellows! C'mon, we'll join 'em."

As they approached the table where John, Rebecca, Cathy, and Derek were enjoying dinner together, their attention was drawn to a table across the room where three male students had erupted in raucous laughter. They were creating quite a ruckus and Donny couldn't help but remark, "Wonder what's so funny that they've gotta annoy everyone else?"

Almost as soon as Donny and David arrived at their friends' table, Derek excused himself, saying he would be right back. Donny's eyebrows shot up quizzically, and he gave Derek a bemused look as he walked away. "Why in the heavens is he leaving? We just got here! Huh! That's a sociable thing to do."

"Oh relax, fussbudget!" said Rebecca. "He's just going over to pick up Jason's food tray."

"Who's Jason?" queried David.

"Jason Portello. He is the boy in the electric wheelchair. Didn't you see him leave?"

"Yes! In fact, he motored right past us! He looked very upset. Why did he leave in such a hurry?"

Cathy nodded toward the other table. "See those three guys over there?"

"The ones making all that noise? We noticed them on our way in. What about them?"

Cathy continued, "See the one in the red ball cap? That's Michael Dervin. I don't know him well, but he's in one of my classes. He thinks he's hot stuff, and he likes to prove it when he's around his friends." Cathy raised the first two fingers of both hands as quotation marks when she said the word *prove*. "He was making fun of Jason. His friends thought it was hilarious and egged him on. Jason left abruptly and didn't even bother taking his tray to the window. That's why Derek is getting it now."

Donny was grinding his teeth when Derek returned with the tray. "Why, I oughta go over there and make *him* cry."

"No, Donald." David's reply was quick. "That's not the Christ-like thing to do here. Reacting in anger would get us nowhere. It makes me angry too, but to respond to that anger would be wrong. Remember, Michael needs Jesus's love as much as anyone else." David's statement was calm but on the inside he was seething. He had lost some of his appetite, and he only half-heartedly picked at his food. His other friends continued conversing and began laughing at Donald's retelling of the wheelchair accident on the way over. But David could not get his mind off Jason. Being in a wheelchair himself, he could definitely relate to the way Jason must have been feeling.

"Are you all right, David?" Derek's question brought him back to the present.

"Yeah, I'm fine. Just thinking."

"You seemed totally lost in thought."

"I was." David did not say anything else, and Derek knew him well enough not to keep probing.

The friends finished their meal and said their good-byes. As Donny pushed David home, he too brought up David's melancholy mood. "What's up, David? Something's really eating at you."

"Yeah," admitted David. "That whole Jason/Michael thing is bothering me."

"Well, don't let it. There's nothing you can do about it right now. Cheer up! You're no fun when you're gloomy."

"Okay, sorry. So how do I cheer up?"

"Think of something funny."

"Like you?" A small, upward curl formed on the edges of David's mouth.

Donny let out a chuckle. "Verrry funny."

David laughed. "Well! You said to think of something funny!"

"Think of something else!" chuckled Donny.

"Hmm. Something else. Oh! I know! Did you hear what Rebecca called you tonight?"

Donny started turning red. "Yes, I did. I was hoping you didn't though."

David was already laughing. "Fussbudget!" He guffawed even more. "That was awesome!" His laughter was contagious and soon Donny was laughing too. They were still chortling as they passed through the gate into their housing complex. As they entered the dorm, they passed two students standing outside. As the door closed behind them, one of the students piped up, "What do you think those two were laughing about?"

The other one responded with a chuckle, "Beats me, Frank! You never know when that rascal Donald Fresnett is involved!"

5

A Decision, a Discovery, and a Diary

The first week was over. *Praise Jesus!* thought David. *I only have one more week in this wheelchair before I get my crutches. I'll sure be ready for that!*

It was Saturday and David was sitting in one of the numerous study lounges scattered across campus. He had found the empty room and decided to try to get some studying done while everyone else was busy, but now that he was there his mind wouldn't focus. Instead, it kept wandering…to Andrea.

It seemed that lately he couldn't get her off his mind. He knew he had to be careful because if he let the relationship go too far, it would become too big of a distraction in his life; but he also knew he had some thinking to do. David knew that technically he was old enough to begin thinking about getting married, but he also knew that God had given him a clear call to minister in whatever way he could to the students at Pinevale. He did not want a relationship with Andrea to get in the way of that.

Currently, he was very satisfied with how things were going at college. He had already gotten together with some of the guys from Dunamis and led some Bible studies through which he was able to pour into their lives. Those moments were so fulfilling that he wanted nothing to distract him from God's work. *But God,* he thought, *why do I have to let that keep me from something else that's good? I love that girl! Why can't I have both?*

David sat there for a moment in confusion when he felt that quiet whisper inside him say, "You want that relationship that you call good, but do you want the good to ruin the *best* that I have for you? I have a perfect plan for you. Will you trust Me enough to wait?" David did not want to hear that...and he definitely did not want to answer those questions. He sat there for a moment in silence, pondering everything. The whisper came again, "Open your Bible."

David had begun carrying his Bible around in his backpack because he never knew when it would come in handy during a discussion. He flipped it open. It opened to 1 Timothy chapter 5, so he started reading. No sooner had he reached the second verse than it jumped off the page at him. He stopped and stared. He read it again, out loud this time, because he couldn't believe what it was saying to him. "Treat the older women as mothers, *and the younger women as sisters, in all purity.*" God was speaking to him about Andrea.

Okay, God, he thought, *I will be careful to guard Andrea's heart and treat her with all purity. I do not want to act in an unbecoming way toward her if she's not truly the one for me. I don't want some guy acting impurely with my future wife, and I surely don't want to do the same with someone else's girl, even if I do think she's the one for me. Now is not the time to play with her feelings. I don't even want to tell her that I love her because it won't do anything but harm right now.* David had just made a heartrending decision, but he knew it was the right one. If God wanted him to marry Andrea, He would work it all out.

━━━►●◄━━━

David looked up as a slender figure stepped into the room. It was Andrea. "How did you know I was here?" he asked in surprise.

"I didn't," she replied. "I happened to be walking by the door and saw you through the window. Whatcha up to?"

"I was just trying to get some studying done."

"Oh. Well then, I'll leave you be. I don't want to interrupt."

"No, no. It's fine. I was getting ready to pack up anyway. I'm headed back to my dorm."

"All right, I'll walk with you that far. Here, let me carry your backpack for you." David wheeled out of the room, and Andrea followed him. "So I heard you were upset about Michael making fun of Jason."

David looked up sharply in surprise. "Who told you that?"

She laughed. "Rebecca."

"Oh yeah," David said, "I forgot that what one of you knows, the other knows too." He grinned.

"That's not a bad thing," Andrea countered, a little defensively.

"No, definitely not. That's not what I meant. In fact, I think it's essential that all young ladies should have another female friend as their confidant—someone they can discuss everything with. That's important. By the way, how did Rebecca know I was so upset? I didn't say anything."

"Oh, she could tell. You'd be surprised what the female species can pick up in members of the opposite sex," Andrea said with a laugh.

"Whatever." David shook his head. "But yes, I was, and I still am very upset. I can relate to Jason since I'm in this wheelchair. In fact, I almost felt his pain. It was so real to me, and it hit very close to home, and I don't even know him."

"I believe that's a good thing, Dave! When you read through the gospel accounts of Jesus's life, you read over and over again how Jesus had compassion for those around Him. He felt compassion many times right before He healed them of their physical and spiritual problems. Compassion is a wonderful thing; it creates a desire to do something for those in need like nothing else I know. Compassion was the driving force of Jesus's ministry, and it should be the driving force of ours."

Andrea stopped as if realizing what she was saying. David was staring at her in disbelief. "Andi..." David stopped, searching for words. "That did not sound like you! I've never heard you talk about spiritual things with such fervor before. And I surely have never heard such wisdom flow from you. Thank you."

Andrea was turning a bit red in embarrassment at the compliment. But she recovered quickly and said, "No, David. Thank you. You are right. I never have been this interested in spiritual things before. But it was you that got me interested." She paused before continuing, "It was that night that Pastor Blake prayed for you. I could tell something had changed in you. That night was the longest night of my life. I wanted what you had, but I didn't want to give up certain things in my life to get it. I had quite a wrestling match with God that night. I had a rough time with it—God won."

——⟫●⟪——

David's heart felt as if it would burst. He had never been so happy before. Knowing that Andrea was in the same boat with him about the whole God thing made him want to sing. Reaching his dorm, he said good-bye to the one he so desperately loved and rushed into his room. Donny came out of the bathroom and almost got knocked over by David scooting past in his wheelchair.

"Whoa! Slow down, big boy! Take it easy on us small fellas! What's the rush anyway?"

"Oh, not much. God is just so good, and I couldn't wait to get to my diary to write all about it."

"That exciting, huh? You'll have to show me once you're done."

Very few people want others reading their personal diaries, but incredibly, David always let Donny read his entries. Donny even knew David was smitten with Andrea. David was close enough with his roommate to share his most intimate thoughts, and the two friends were able to spiritually support each other. For all of Donny's antics, he could really be a deep and thoughtful person.

Half an hour later, Donny's struggle with homework was interrupted by David's notebook being slid under his nose. He picked it up and began to read.

> *Jim Elliott, the missionary to Ecuador who was murdered by the Auca Indians, once said, 'He is no fool who gives what he cannot keep to gain what he cannot lose.' Jim is talking about your life. It could be rewritten as "He is no fool who gives his life to gain Life." Life with a capital L is talking about eternal life, spiritual*

life, real life. I was a fool for a long time. I didn't want to give my life for the things of God. But this is what Jesus was addressing when he said, "For whoever wishes to save his life will lose it; but whoever loses his life for My sake will find it." (Matthew 16:25)

When I finally gave up my whole life for the things of God, it was a liberating experience. I knew I didn't have to worry about anything because God would take care of it all. But I knew it would be hard. I knew I would be lonely at times and feel as if no one else cared for the things of God. But oh, how good God is!

The girl I love has just admitted to me that my new life in Christ tugged at something in her heart and that she wanted to have that same thing in her life. She said something to me today that I never heard her say before. There was a new sense of wisdom, understanding, and sincerity to her words that wasn't there previously. It is so exciting to me that the special one God has brought into my life has felt the same urgency that I have to live for the purposes of our Savior King. Praise be to the King of kings and Lord of lords, Maker of heaven and earth!"

Donny looked up with a raised eyebrow and a slight grin. "So Andrea's caught the bug too, huh? Does she know how happy she made you?"

"Yes, somewhat. I don't know if she knows the full extent of it though." David smiled. "I told her I was proud of her.

Actually, come to think of it, right before that, she told me I would be surprised at what the female gender can pick up in members of the opposite sex. She probably does know how happy I am."

"Well, whether she does or not, Dave, I'm happy for you," said Donny. "I'm really happy for you."

6

CONFRONTATION AND CRUTCHES

It was Monday. Another week had begun. David had just gotten out of his first class. He had an hour until the next one, so he decided to get something to eat. Wheeling himself to the main cafeteria, he began to pick up lunch items. He had become better at accomplishing this process while in a wheelchair. It still took some time, but at least it went a little smoother. He ordered a burger and balanced the lunch tray on his lap, grabbing some fries and a bottle of water. Taking it slower now, he made his way to the checkout where he paid for the items and rolled out into the cafeteria's seating area. He headed toward his favorite corner of the room where it was generally a little quieter. One factor that played a role in this peace was the fact that there were no televisions blaring overhead. But as David neared the corner, he saw that all was not quiet today. Pulled up to a table was Jason Portello in his electric wheelchair. This was the student that had been crying as he zipped passed David and Donny on his way out of The Kitchen a few days earlier. Standing behind him was Michael Dervin, the loud student who had been making fun of Jason. Michael was jamming the wheelchair into the table and pulling it back out so that Jason couldn't get situated the right distance from the table. Michael was laughing at Jason's futile attempts to position his wheelchair with his controls.

Anger exploded inside David. Once again, he clearly felt the pain and hurt that Jason was experiencing. He placed his tray on a table and wheeled up behind Michael. In a low but confident and firm voice seething with righteous anger, he said, "Michael, let go of him."

Michael's sneer disappeared as he whipped around to see who had spoiled his fun. He began snickering when he saw it was another boy in a wheelchair. "Who are you? And why should I listen to you?" he asked.

"Because, Michael, I won't put up with it. If you continue harassing Jason, I will take it to the school authorities."

Michael seemed to notice for the first time that David had said his name. "How do you know my name? And who *are* you?"

"It doesn't matter," replied David. "Now get out of here!" His eyes flashed like fire.

Michael paused as if pondering whether he should let himself be bossed around by a kid in a wheelchair.

"Now!" David was losing his temper fast with this bully, and his interjection cut through Michael's hesitation.

After momentarily staring at David's eyes, Michael began walking away, but he looked back with a scowl on his face and said, "Listen up, Bud. Nobody talks to Michael Dervin like that. You're lucky you're in a wheelchair or I wouldn't be taking that from you. You and I will meet again!" He turned and walked away.

David muttered under his breath, "Yes, I'm sure we probably will." Then aloud he called out, "Michael, wait!"

Michael turned around with a quizzical look on his face. David held his eyes for a moment before saying in a level voice, "Michael, God loves you." Michael's look of astonishment appeared before he could do anything to control it. Slowly, his face turned red and then purple with livid anger. Somehow he managed to control the words choking in his throat before abruptly turning and stomping out of the room.

David watched Michael's back as he exited through the cafeteria doors before turning to face Jason. "Hello, friend," he said with a smile.

Jason looked confused. "I'll ask the same question that he just asked you," he said, nodding toward the doors through which Michael had just disappeared. "Who are you? Not only did you call Michael by his name, but you also mentioned my name, and I've never met you! How do you know me?"

David's smile broadened as he extended his hand across the table and shook Jason's hand. "I'm David Pearl. I've seen you around campus, but I didn't know your name until last week. I saw you rush out of The Kitchen, and there were some friends of mine who had seen what happened between you and Michael. They told me all about it. One of them is apparently in a class with you and another knew Michael's name too."

Jason looked embarrassed when David mentioned his other run-in with Michael. David noticed this and quickly changed the subject. "Hold on a moment, Jason. Let me get my lunch tray and I'll join you." After retrieving his lunch, David said, "I don't mean to be nosy, but would you mind telling me about yourself?"

"Well, there's not much to tell really," he replied. "I'm a sophomore, and I'm here to study communication. I'm the second of two children. My brother, Jim, is a sergeant first class in the marines. He was awarded the Medal of Honor for saving his platoon. He was always athletic and outgoing when we were growing up. I've always tried to measure up to Jim in any way I can, but this darn wheelchair has ruined my life. I was crippled from birth." Jason spit out the last sentence with bitter disappointment. "The only thing that I was ever decent at was shooting competitively with the pistol. I could shoot just as well or better than Jim, but that's it. Other than that, I can't do much of anything."

David felt an overwhelming sense of pity for Jason. "You know," he said. "You don't have to measure your life against your brother's or anyone else's for that matter. You are unique, and God has a specific purpose for your life. He wants to give you joy and a purpose for living if you'll only trust Him."

Jason scowled. "Don't talk to me about God," he muttered. "God doesn't love me. If He did, I wouldn't be in this wheelchair, always taking the brunt of everyone's jokes."

"Listen, Jason, I'm sure I can't fully relate to your situation as I've only been in this wheelchair a short time. But you'd better believe that I was quite despondent when I was confined to this contraption. Through it all, God has stayed true to me, and I've learned how to cope with it and find joy even though I'm in the middle of a bad situation. He wants to do the same with you."

Jason still didn't look convinced, but he was not frowning anymore. "Look," said David, "I've got to run. I have another class in twenty minutes, and it will take me a while to get there, but I'll see you around. We'll hang out some more. It was nice meeting you, Jason!"

Jason managed a small grin. "Yes, it was nice meeting you too, David. And thanks for what you did today. I get so upset with that bully, I just don't know what to do. Thanks a lot!"

David waved it off. "No problem! Have a great day, and God bless!"

———◆———

Jason watched David as he slowly wheeled himself from the cafeteria. He shook his head. He could not tell what it was, but something was different about David; something he liked. He had something that was genuine, something that was alive!

One thing that had really struck him about David was his eyes. Although dark brown, they seemed to be as clear as glass when David spoke about God. It was almost as if Jason could see deep down into them, the whole way down to David's heart. There was an emotion in those eyes that Jason could not define, an emotion that he didn't know. He had not experienced it for many years. Even though he could not put his finger on it, Jason liked it; all of it. The boy, the eyes, and the unnamed emotion.

Unknown to Jason, the emotion that shone through David's eyes did have a name; it was called love.

—————

Finally! Two weeks had passed and David was sitting in the doctor's office. Doctor Mallory looked up from the x-rays and seemed pleased. "This has healed up, ah, very nicely! Very nicely! You still er, want to, ahem, be quite careful with it though. Quite careful indeed!" It seemed as though Doctor Mallory had picked up another annoying habit on top of his already hesitating speech. Now, rarely did a sentence come out of his mouth that he didn't repeat the last few words.

Dr. Mallory had cut the cast off and replaced it with a removable walking cast that would allow David to have a bit more mobility. Equipped with a new set of crutches, David tentatively tried a few steps. It didn't feel too bad! David stopped and lowered his injured foot to the ground. Unfortunately, he didn't do it gently enough, and it bounced against the floor with a jolt. David winced. He could now appreciate why the doc had said he still needed to be careful with his leg.

After a few more instructions from the stuttering doctor, David hobbled out to the waiting room. Donny poked his nose up above the magazine he had been reading. A grin crept across his face. "So you did get your crutches, Davy! Now I can call you Three-Legs!"

David snorted. "If I hear you calling me Three-Legs, your name will forever be Sore-Tush from the red welt I leave across your bottom with one of these crutches! Come on. Let's get back to campus!"

⟶⟫●⟪⟵

Never had David felt as grateful as he did in obtaining his new set of crutches. It was pure bliss to get around on his own without a set of wheels beneath him. Obviously, the crutches got in the way, but it was definitely an improvement. He was still quite clumsy with them, but he didn't care. Unable to sit still, David hobbled over to the library, which was the second closest building to his dorm. One corner of the quiet building had two comfy armchairs that were especially cozy for reading. He had bumped into

Andrea there numerous times and was hoping that she would be there now so he could share his good news with her. Entering the library, he had to walk by the stairs that led to the second floor. Ruefully, he eyed them knowing that before his accident he used to bound up them two or three steps at a time. Now he had to take the elevator. *Oh well,* he thought. *It's just for a season.*

If Andrea was there, David wanted to surprise her, so nearing the corner in question, he ducked between two bookshelves and worked his way forward until there was only one bookshelf between him and the armchairs. This bookshelf had a back so he couldn't see through it, but David could hear a conversation taking place on the other side. It was indeed Andrea, and it sounded as if she was conversing with a girl from Dunamis. Listening intently, David could just barely hear what she was saying. When he did hear, he was overjoyed!

"The Bible says that everything God created was good. You are beautiful, and you were made for a reason. Those thoughts that encourage low self-esteem are from the devil." There was a pause. The other girl did not seem convinced, so Andrea continued. "I just read in the Bible this morning a passage in First John that might apply to this. Let me find it." David heard pages rustling. If he had been surprised at first, he was even more flabbergasted now. The fact that Andrea had actually brought her Bible with her to the library was amazing. She had definitely changed!

"Here it is. 1 John 3:19–20 says that our heart condemns us but that we are to assure our heart before God because He is greater than our heart and He knows all things. Also, Proverbs says that people become what they think. The more you entertain these thoughts, the more you will start to believe them. You must wage war on them! Every time you find yourself thinking those things, you need to say, 'No! I am a child of Christ. I was bought with a price! I am a new creation! The old has gone and the new has come! No longer do I believe that I am not beautiful. No longer do I believe that I have no worth! I am a daughter of the Most High God!'"

The other girl spoke for the first time. David thought she was a freshman. "All right." Then she sighed. "I'll try. But it's just so hard!"

"I know it is," Andrea agreed in a comforting tone of voice. "I know it is. But you can definitely do it! I believe in you! Besides, God will be with you through your entire struggle. You can do it, girl!"

"I'll try, that's for sure. I guess I better get going. Thanks so much, Andrea! I really needed to hear that!" As the two friends said good-bye, David slowly backed away. Again, he felt a feeling of overwhelming joy to know that Andrea had definitely caught a hunger for the Lord. But he did not want to let her know he had heard the conversation. It was not because he felt guilty for eavesdropping. He had no problem admitting *that* to her. But it was because he was still being careful to guard the relationship between the two of them. If he told Andrea that he had heard everything and that he was proud of her again, it would only make both of them feel even more attracted to each other. As hard as it was to accept, David knew that was not a good thing to do right now. Emerging from the bookshelves, David walked straight toward Andrea's location as if walking through the library for the first time. Walking past the end of the last shelf, he caught Andrea's gaze and looked startled as if surprised to see her there. Then he grinned. He could definitely be quite the actor when he wanted to be.

7

MYSTERIOUS WAYS

It was Friday. Another week had passed, and David was adjusting well to his crutches. Today he had arranged to eat with Derek, the student president of Dunamis. Tomorrow was Andrea's birthday, and the two of them were working out details for a surprise party for her. They had already decided to go to a roller rink because skating was one of her favorite activities. This would leave David sitting on the sidelines, but he didn't mind; that's what Andrea liked to do so that's what he wanted to do.

Derek and David had decided to meet at a small dining unit located in one corner of campus instead of at the main cafeteria. To get there, David had to walk along a less-traveled sidewalk. It was actually two sidewalks that ran parallel to each other with a tall hedge between them. They were connected at fairly frequent intervals by crosswalks that cut through the hedge. David swung along on his crutches, enjoying the fresh spring air and listening to the chatter of the songbirds in the hedge.

Suddenly, the serenity of the setting was broken by the sound of raised voices on the other side of the hedge. One said, "Just knock it off! Let me go!" This was followed by a loud snicker from a second person.

Immediately, David knew Jason and Michael were at it again. He took large strides on his crutches as he rushed back to the break in the hedge he had just passed and crossed to the other sidewalk. His guess was confirmed as he saw the figure of Michael standing in the path of Jason's wheelchair. They were about twenty feet from where David stood. He did not go any closer to them but spoke with words that sped like arrows of ice to Michael's unprotected back. "Get out of his way, Michael!" For the second time, Michael spun away from his prey to see David Pearl staring at him with eyes of fire.

Shocked to see him again, Michael stuttered, "How... wha....? What are you doing here again, church boy?" He said "church boy" with a sneer but quickly looked at the ground and cursed under his breath, intimidated by David's relentless gaze. *How in the world could this snotty kid have such dangerous eyes?*

"It doesn't matter what I'm doing here," came David's curt answer. "The question is what are you doing here? I told you to stay away from Jason." David glanced behind Michael to see Jason racing off in the opposite direction.

He had taken the opportunity to escape when David confronted Michael. No matter, David would catch up with him later.

Turning back to Michael, David saw an expression of the wildest hate he had ever seen flash from the antagonist's face. For all of his apparent confidence, David still shuddered internally when he saw it; it was pure evil. Outwardly, David kept his cool and returned Michael's gaze. It was not long until Michael looked down and slowly started walking toward David. As he did, he muttered, "Okay, I'm leaving now, but don't think I'm just going to keep taking all this crap from some church boy."

Without answering, David moved to the side of the walk and proceeded in the direction he had been traveling, which was toward Michael. As they came abreast of each other, Michael drew back his leg and, putting his whole body into it, swiftly kicked David's crutch as hard as he could. The crutch spun up into the air, creating a massive arc before plummeting to the earth fifteen feet away.

David was in mid-swing when his crutch was forcibly wrenched out from under his arm. As his body crumpled toward the ground, he instinctively tried to maintain his balance. Without thinking, he extended his hurt leg to catch himself. The instant his foot came in contact with the earth, his mind realized what he had done, and he gasped, knowing the pain that was to follow. In a flash, he remembered several times when he slightly banged his leg against things when he was in the walking cast. That hurt enough, but with all his weight coming down on that weak leg, he knew that he was probably going to break it again.

There was an audible snap. He hit the ground and instinctively cried out, expecting pain to come shooting up his leg, but there was none. He lay still, thinking that maybe his leg was just numb from the shock, but slowly he began to realize that he was not in shock, that his leg was not numb, and that he indeed felt no pain. In fact, his leg felt amazingly good! It felt…normal! It felt whole! It felt strong! Amazed, it slowly began to dawn on him that the snap he had heard was not his leg breaking, but that it was his broken bones being knit together! It was a weird moment. He didn't know how he knew it, but he knew he was completely healed! God had done a miracle! Seizing the Velcro on his walking cast, he ripped it off and without waiting to test his weight, jumped off the ground and landed on his feet. No pain! He jumped up and down several times on the previously injured leg. No pain! Next, he ran over to a nearby tree and banged the side of his leg against the trunk. No pain! A minute ago this would have caused excruciating pain.

When Michael first kicked the crutch, he hit it so hard that tears popped unbidden from his eyes as he hopped around on one foot, hoping the pain would subside. Then he noticed David and, forgetting the pain in his own foot, stood with his mouth open wide as he watched David's movements. At first, he thought David had hit his head on the ground when he fell and now he was a little loco. But after seeing the look of ecstatic joy on David's face, he knew that wasn't the case. He couldn't understand how this boy with the broken leg could do what he was seeing him do.

David's shout reached him. "Praise Jesus! I'm healed! I'm healed! Michael, thank you! I'm healed!" David began running toward Michael, but the astounded student backed away with his hands up.

"I don't know what just happened," he stuttered, his eyes wide with fear. "But stay away from me. Get back!"

David kept coming with a smile on his face. "Look, Michael! God used you to heal me! I can walk!" But Michael couldn't handle it any longer and he turned and ran. David's shout followed him, "Michael, wait!" Michael didn't stop or turn around to see what David had to say, so David shouted after the fleeing figure, "Michael! God loves you!" Beaming, he watched Michael disappear around a corner.

Rarely was his smile so big. He retrieved the cast and the two crutches, and breaking into a run, made his way toward his meeting with Derek. He was late, but he didn't care. It felt so good to run on his own two feet with the wind whipping in his ears! He couldn't believe what had happened! God was too good for words to describe!

<hr />

David burst into the dining unit and ran up to the table where Derek was sitting. Derek looked up and his jaw dropped. "What? How in the world are you able to walk without the aid of your crutches?"

David laughed at the astounded look on his friend's face and said, "Well, you and I believe in a God who heals, and guess what? He's still in the business!" David ordered a quick sandwich and between bites told the Dunamis president how it had happened.

When he finished, Derek shook his head and said, "Wow. That's all I can say. Wow! I can't believe it. It's incredible! God sure does work in mysterious ways."

"I know!" replied David. "I can't believe it myself. I can walk! It's crazy!"

After running over a few details concerning the surprise party for Andrea, David said, "Look, I don't like cutting this short and I'd love to stay and talk some more, but after what happened, I just have to tell some other people and call my parents. I'm too excited."

Derek agreed, "Sure thing, bro! I would too if I was in your shoes. You can't keep news like that to yourself! Get out there and let me know what people say when you tell them!"

David thanked him and then said, "One more thing. If you happen to bump into Andrea, don't tell her what happened. I'm going to turn that surprise party of hers tomorrow into a *real* surprise!"

After an acknowledging grin from Derek, he turned and began walking away. As he did, he happened to see out of the corner of his eye a young student get up from a table a short distance away and approach Derek. The student introduced himself and David heard him say, "Excuse me, I couldn't help but overhear your conversation and I'm confused about what's going on. You said that God healed that guy, but that's not possible, is it? I mean, I'd think you both were crazy except that I've seen that guy in a wheelchair and on crutches, and I know that his leg was broken. But how is he walking? Can you explain that?"

David turned and caught Derek's eye. He smiled. God was already using this miracle to further His kingdom. Now Derek had a perfect opportunity to share God's love with this student. David turned and walked out as he heard Derek begin to share truth with this young man who was missing the most important thing in his life: God.

———⊳●⊲———

Donald Fresnett was finally getting out of his two-hour statistics class. He stumbled into his room and dropped his overstuffed backpack on the floor. "Whew! Glad to be done with that! That's one humdinger of a class!"

David was sitting at his desk, writing in his journal. He had put his cast back on, and his crutches were leaning up against the desk beside him. He swiveled around in his chair, being careful not to bang the cast against the desk and, looking at Donny with a sly smile on his face, said, "Hey Donny, go get your jump rope. I want to see your tricks." Donny was an expert at jumping rope. David was amazed at the speed with which he swung the rope and his fancy footwork. In fact, Donny did it on a regular basis for exercise.

Donny's eyebrows knotted together. "What for? You never ask me to do that in the middle of the day."

David's face was a picture of innocence as he answered, "No reason, I just feel like seeing you do it. Besides, you need a diversion to clear your mind from that 'humdinger of a class' you just got out of."

"Yeah, I'll agree to that." Donny nodded as he fetched the rope out of his closet. Standing in the middle of the room, he started swinging the rope, slowly at first and then faster and faster. As he warmed up to the exercise, he began hopping on one foot and then the other, spinning in a circle and crossing his hands.

Suddenly, David stopped him. "Here, let me see that rope. I want to try that."

Donny looked at him like his head was upside down. "Yeah, right! Dude! You're on crutches! You can't jump rope!"

David shook his head. "I'm sick of being tied down to these things. Besides, my leg feels really, really good today. Give me the rope."

Donny slowly handed it over. He looked dubiously at the cast on David's leg. "You complain when you just bump your leg against something, and now you want to jump up and down and put all your weight on it! This doesn't make sense. Your leg hurts you even when your cast is on!"

David looked up. "Well I'm definitely not wearing my cast to jump rope! It's too bulky. It would definitely get in the way. I'd trip and do a face plant. Then I'd need a cast on my skull." And with that, he reached down and began undoing the Velcro on his walking boot.

Now Donny was really distressed. "Dave! You can't do that! You can't put all your weight on that leg!"

But David pretended to ignore him, and before Donny could do anything to stop him, he stood up, faked a slight limp to the middle of the room, and began to jump rope. Of course, he couldn't do it as fast or as fancily as Donny had, but judging by the look on Donny's face, David figured he was more than astounded.

Donny was speechless. David stopped and laughed out loud at the look on Donny's face. "I...I don't know what to say," Donny stuttered in amazement.

"That's a first." David chuckled.

"But how...? How are you able to do that?" squeaked out Donny.

David inhaled and, filling his lungs to full capacity, he yelled, "*I'm healed!*" He stamped his previously broken foot hard on the floor for emphasis and rushed over to where his roommate stood. He grabbed him around the waist, picked him up off the floor, and began spinning around yelling, "I'm healed, Donny! I can walk! I can run! I'm healed! God healed me!"

Donny could not believe what was happening, but he managed to spit out, "Okay, ya great big lug! Let go of me! Oof! Put me down, this instant! You're squeezing the guts outta me! Yah!"

David abruptly stopped and dropped his friend unexpectedly. Unable to get his feet under him, Donny dropped to the floor like a sack of grain. Looking up with a wry expression on his face, he said, "Not like that, you great big goober! Now you've not only broken every one of my ribs but cracked my tailbone too!" Then he jumped up spryly and said, "Well, come on, Davy, quit smirking. Tell me the story! How did it happen? Tell me!"

8

SURPRISE

The following day dawned bright and sunny. David's heart leapt within him the moment he awoke as he remembered the events of the previous day. God's love was so amazing, and all he could do was live in awe of the amazing might and sovereignty of his wonderful Savior!

He jumped out of bed and did a little jig on the bedroom floor, reveling in his newfound freedom. Waltzing over to Donny's bed, he tickled his roommate and shouted, "Wakey, wakey, buddy! It's a bee-utiful day!"

No answer. Donny lay still as he tried in vain to ignore his friend's words. "Come on, Donald! As good old Ben Franklin said, 'Early to bed, early to rise, makes a man healthy, wealthy, and wise.' So what are you waiting for? It's time to rise and shine!"

Donny grunted but continued to lie still, then groggily he retorted, "I'll rise and give you a shiner! Man, Dave!

You're worse than a rooster that got his clock knocked forward two hours!"

David just laughed and ripped off another quote, "Remember, the early bird gets the worm, Donny!"

Donald grunted again. "Ooh. Such an incentive! I can't wait to get up now!"

David had heard enough. He tore back the sheets saying, "Okay, buddy, if you don't get up, I'm going to pour water down your ear!"

Donny didn't believe him and let out a fake snore as he feigned sleep. David tiptoed to the bathroom and filled a cup with water. Coming back, he dribbled a few drops into Donny's upturned right ear and quickly jumped back to watch the explosion.

"*Yaaah!* I didn't think you'd actually do it!" roared Donny as he sat straight up in bed, poking and rubbing at his ear. "You big rascal you!"

David was laughing so hard he could barely speak, but he grabbed his pillow and managed to utter, "Here, let me help you get that water out of your ear!" And with that, he gave the left side of Donny's head a mighty thump with his pillow. Donny pretended to almost fall off the bed with the impact but came up in an instant with his pillow flying. After a good beating, both of them decided they had had enough.

David scoffed. "It worked! I got you out of bed." Donny just rolled his eyes. But a few minutes later, when David was bent over his bed trying to make some order of the rumpled sheets, Donny got the last jab. Taking one last mighty swing with his pillow, he sent dust flying off David's rump.

⎯⎯⎯▶●◀⎯⎯⎯

All the plans were set for the evening. A mass e-mail had been sent out to all the members of Dunamis, telling them to show up at the roller rink by 6:30 p.m. They had rented the rink for the night and Andrea thought that Rebecca was taking her out to eat.

David decided that he would try to get some homework done before the party, so he set out for the library. He desperately hoped that he would not run into Andrea. He wanted to really surprise her this evening. As he walked, David remembered trying to get Donny to go running with him again that morning. With a laugh, he recalled Donny's reply. "No way are you getting me to run with you, buster! After getting your leg healed, you're going to be itching to run faster than ever! I'd never keep up!"

"Aw! Come on!" said David. "It's because I haven't run for several weeks that I'll be going slower. I'm out of shape!"

"Not that much," came the reply. "Besides, you've waited too long now. The sun's too high in the sky. I'd melt away to nothing in this heat, and the flies would be worse than ever!"

⎯⎯⎯▶●◀⎯⎯⎯

Just outside the library, David bumped into none other than Jason Portello. When Jason saw David, his eyes widened in disbelief. "David! You're walking without crutches! I don't understand! How are you doing that?"

David looked at the boy who had been confined to a wheelchair from birth and had to wonder why God had decided to heal him and not Jason. He just didn't have answers to those questions, but he trusted God and knew that the Lord was in control.

Outwardly, he smiled at Jason and said, "Hello, friend! I've got a lot to tell you! Where are you headed?"

"Oh, nowhere in particular. I just got done studying. Were you headed to the library?"

"Yes," replied David, "but there was nothing super urgent that I had to do. Do you mind if we find a nice, shady spot on campus and have a chat?"

Jason agreed and the two proceeded down the walk to a small grove of shade trees in the middle of campus. It had benches scattered around with several small fountains in the middle. David took a seat on one of the benches, and Jason pulled his wheelchair in front of it. "Okay," he demanded. "Tell me how you're walking. I just don't get it. You can't do that! Your leg is broken!"

David smiled. "Not anymore it's not. It happened the other day when I met you and Michael on the sidewalk. In fact, you just missed it when you zoomed off. I had talked with Michael a bit more, but of course he got mad at me. He was headed in the opposite direction and when he passed me, he kicked one of my crutches out from under me. I was unprepared and put all my weight down on my bad foot. The rest I'm not sure you'll believe, but it's the truth. I heard a snap and thought I was re-breaking my leg, but after a few moments, I realized that that wasn't the case. In fact, my leg felt really good! I stood up and my leg was completely healed, Jason! God miraculously healed me! And He used Michael to do it! It was incredible!"

As David told what had happened, Jason was in disbelief, and he had no problem saying so. "I can't believe that. That's just not possible!"

"I'm still having trouble believing it myself," responded David. "But it definitely happened. If you don't believe me, just ask Michael." David stopped and laughed. "Michael was totally shocked when it happened. In fact, he was freaked out. He wouldn't let me come near him. When I walked toward him, he turned and ran!"

Jason managed a small chuckle, but then turned sober again. "David. I'm going to be serious with you. I want to believe it. I really do. I want to believe it, but I just haven't seen God work in my life like that. Besides, that kind of stuff doesn't happen today, does it? I mean, come on! Any doctor will tell you that's impossible!"

"Yes, it is impossible—if you look at it from a human perspective. But with God, all things are possible. He made me in the first place, so surely he knows how to fix me! And yes, miracles do still happen today. You need to read through the Bible. Jesus healed many, many people. He made the blind to see, the deaf to hear, and the lame to walk, even though they had been lame from birth, just like you! He healed them all. Jesus was the Son of God, which in fact, made him God. The Bible says that He is the same yesterday, today, and forever, which means that He can still heal people today! And He does! I'm living evidence of that!"

Jason still seemed doubtful, but less noticeably so. "I don't know, David. I just don't know. You can't expect me to believe in something or someone who has never proven himself to me, otherwise, I could never know that it is real."

David shook his head. God is showing Himself to you all the time. You've just got to open your eyes and look. Besides, Jesus said, 'Blessed are those who have not seen Me and yet have believed.' It's called faith, Jason. You can believe in Him if you want. He will not let you down. Besides, this is your only life. You only get to live it once, and then it's done. If you miss it now, you've missed it forever."

———◆———

Andrea was humming contentedly to herself as she headed over to Rebecca's dorm room. Rebecca was taking her out to dinner for her birthday this evening, and Andrea was supposed to meet her in her room at six o'clock. Andrea had been having an excellent day, considering it was a Saturday and she didn't have any classes. But one thought nagged her—why had she not seen or heard anything from David

Pearl? It was not like him to forget about her birthday, and she couldn't imagine that he didn't feel like talking to her. Earlier she had considered trying to find him, but then decided that she would just wait and see what happened. It still bothered her though. She wanted to share this day with him.

Entering the dormitory, Andrea climbed the flight of stairs to Rebecca's second floor hallway and knocked on Rebecca's door.

"Come in!" came her friend's cheery voice.

Andrea opened the door a crack and poked her head in. "It's just me!"

Rebecca turned from her desk where she was seated and smiled. "Yeah, I know, Andi!" Andrea entered the room and Rebecca continued, "Oh, and please don't be alarmed at the other person in the room. He's here to help me…with you!"

When Rebecca first said there was someone else in the room, Andrea looked around in surprise at the empty room. But just as she heard the words "with you," she turned around to see a masked figure behind the door that she had just come through. She gasped silently as the figure came toward her with a black cloth bag but realized it must be one of her friends when Rebecca's hand settled on her shoulder. "It's okay, Andi. He's just helping me out. And you might as well know, I'm not taking you to dinner tonight." She laughed. "It's a surprise where you're going, so stand still!"

With that, the masked figure raised the cloth bag and lowered it over Andrea's head. They tied it loosely beneath her chin so she could breathe. Then, in silence, she was led from the room.

⟫●⟪

After getting in the car, Rebecca talked nonstop. Andrea was trying to figure out which way they were going but had some trouble because she had sensed that as soon as the car had been started, they had driven in a circle for a few minutes in the parking lot. She had no clue which way they had come out. Still, she tried to keep track of the turns they made.

Rebecca's last few words filtered through her confused mind. "Isn't that right, Andrea?"

Andrea's muffled response came floating through the cloth bag. "What?"

Rebecca laughed. "I bet you haven't heard anything I said, silly! You've been trying to figure out where we are! Well, I guess you'll find out soon enough, isn't that right, mystery man?" There was no reply. Andrea realized that no sound had come from the masked figure who had blindfolded her. For some reason, they wanted his identity kept secret. She could not imagine who in the world he was.

Finally, after what seemed like hours, the car slowed down and pulled into what Andrea guessed was a parking lot. Sure enough, the engine shut off and she heard Rebecca say, "We're here! Do you know where we are, Andi?"

Andrea shook her head. She was completely lost. Rebecca just laughed and grabbed her friend by the arm to guide her into the building. Andrea felt the air change as she was led inside. They walked straight ahead and made no turns to the right or the left. Everything was quiet; almost too quiet. Andrea had a hunch that they were not alone. She realized she was walking on what seemed to be a very smooth floor. Suddenly, Rebecca stopped, turned Andrea around, and slowly guided her body down into a chair. She then walked behind the chair and said, "Okay, here we are." She paused then yelled, "One…two…*three!*" And with that she yanked the bag off of Andrea's head.

"*Surprise!*" The sudden roar interrupted the previous silence like a train rushing through a quiet valley. Andrea jumped as she suddenly was able to see all her friends from Dunamis. A smile leapt to her lips, and she laughed out loud as she lifted her hands to her swiftly beating heart.

"Oh my goodness! I…I…" Speechless, she stopped. Everyone was laughing and cheering. Looking around, Andrea immediately noticed two things. The first thing she realized was where she was; she was seated in a chair in the middle of the local roller skating rink. The second thing she realized was that David and his crutches were nowhere to be seen among all her friends from Dunamis. She did not know why she realized that so fast, but it was just a fleeting thought as she was confronted by Rebecca, who was now standing in front of her.

"Thank you so much!" Andrea managed to gasp out.

Rebecca beamed, "Don't thank me yet, I still have one more surprise for you." She moved aside, and Andrea saw her group of friends part in the middle as the masked figure who had kidnapped her walked slowly forward. Everyone fell quiet. Andrea felt like she was in the middle of a movie. The suspense was incredible, but she didn't know why. She still had no clue who this man was. She couldn't think of any of her friends who had that build. And why was Rebecca playing this up so much? She glanced over at her friend but only received the smile that was so typical of Rebecca.

She looked back at the masked figure, now only two paces away. She felt her heart beating rapidly and wondered why she was sitting in this chair. She felt so vulnerable. The mystery man's hand rose, and as the mask rose above the man's chin, Andrea suddenly realized who it was. There stood the smiling David Pearl that Andrea used to know—standing proud and tall on his own two feet. Andrea shrieked, and flying out of her seat threw her arms around her friend. David was taken aback for a second but held her for an almost undetectable moment before slowly stepping back from her.

Andrea looked up at him and whispered, "How?" David did not need to respond. His eyes told the whole story.

———❖———

It was Wednesday of the following week, and as Andrea left her last class she was still thinking about the night of her birthday. Forever locked in her memory was the look in David's eyes when she had asked him how he was able to walk. They had been clearer and brighter than she ever remembered seeing them. Instinctively, she had somehow known that he had been miraculously healed. That was enough for her at the moment, but later that night she had asked David for details as they skated around the rink. He had recounted the full story to her and recalled with a laugh Michael's consternation.

"I've never been so…so…joyful!" she told him. "I can't say that I'm happy because the feeling that I have right now is so much more than happiness. It's wonderful!"

David looked at her. "I know, but life is not always going to be bright and shining as it is now. You will not see miracles happen in every circumstance. There will be times when it seems as if God is very distant and unresponsive to things happening in your life. There will be times when life is just the opposite of tonight, times when you have no reason to celebrate. But remember what this joy feels like, keep it close to you. We are to rejoice always, in everything. Stay joyful, Andrea!"

"I will do my best," she had promised.

A shout brought Andrea out of her reverie. She looked down the sidewalk to see Rebecca running to catch up with her. "How are you?" she panted.

Andrea smiled. "Joyful!"

Rebecca grinned back. "Good! Let's go eat!"

"Okay! Are you ready for the Dunamis Spring Retreat this weekend?"

"Absolutely!" replied Rebecca. "I can't wait!" Every spring, Dunamis had a retreat which involved the Christian student groups from several surrounding colleges. It was held after spring break, but before finals started. Usually the retreat was held at an old camp in the mountains near Pinevale. Furnished cabins were available for the students' use.

"What are you looking forward to the most?"

Andrea thought for a bit. "Eh…just everything. The worship, the teaching, and just hanging out with people. It's always neat to get to know some students from the other colleges a bit better."

Rebecca looked sideways at her friend with a coy look on her face. "I guess I know who you'll be hanging out with the most! I saw how you jumped into his arms Saturday night!"

Andrea feigned innocence. "I don't know what you're talking about."

Rebecca just laughed. "Sure you don't."

Andrea smiled. "Okay, I'm not going to deny that. But I need you to know something, Becky. Yes, I'm attracted to David. And I'm ninety-nine percent sure he's also attracted to me—"

Rebecca interrupted. "Ninety-nine percent sure? What are you talking about? It's written all over his face! You don't see that?"

"Well, I guess a little. But I don't think I can see it as well as other people. Anyhow, as I was saying, Saturday was the first time that we even came close to hugging each other. And it's not going to be the norm. In fact, David talked to me that night and asked me not to hug him like that again." Andrea blushed a bit. "I wasn't hugging him because I'm attracted to him. I was simply so overjoyed to see him walking around unhindered on his own two feet that I couldn't help myself. I actually don't even remember how I got to him so fast. All I remember is that I had my arms around him before I knew what had happened."

Rebecca looked surprised. "He actually asked you to not hug him? What kind of guy does that?"

"He's living for purity, and he doesn't want others to read too much into our friendship right now, because that's what it is. At this point we're not in a relationship. That might be in our future, but I'm following David's lead on this. Until he asks me, I'm just going to keep getting to know him as well as I can. I know he doesn't want anything to get in the way of his walk with God, and I certainly don't want to distract him. Sometimes it's really hard for me to accept. I don't want to have to restrain myself, but I love him so much! I want to do what is right because of David but mostly because of God. I want to stay pure in His sight too. So, Becky, can you do me a favor?"

Rebecca nodded. "Sure."

"Please don't act as if we're in a relationship or insinuate that to others, okay? I don't want David to think that I'm talking and acting like we're in a relationship, because we're not. And if it ever does happen, we're going to go about it in as pure and godly a way as possible."

Rebecca smiled. "You can trust me. I won't say anything to inflame the situation. I'll be anxious to see how it works out though."

———⊰●⊱———

On the other side of campus, David had bumped into Michael Dervin. Michael had tried to escape without being seen, but David stopped him and said, "Hey, Michael! I want to talk with you for a sec."

Michael grimaced. "Well, I don't want to talk to you."

David ignored this rude comment and grinned. "Sorry to scare you the other day. I just wanted to talk to you. How are you doing?"

"It doesn't matter, and I told you I don't want to talk to you."

David put it to him honestly, "Michael, I'm not going to beat around the bush. I'm going to tell you straight up. You can keep trying to get me upset, you can keep being rude, and you can keep trying to get rid of me. But I'm telling you, I'm here to be your friend. I will continue to care for you and be your friend until you decide to ask me why."

The two stood in silence as Michael studied David. Then just to get David off his case and make him happy, Michael narrowed his eyes and said, "Okay then, I'll ask just to get you off my back. Why do you want to be my friend?"

"Because I care for you."

"But why?" exploded Michael.

"Michael, let me ask you a question. If you were to die tonight, do you know where you would go? Do you know what would happen to you?"

Michael scowled fiercely and turned to walk away. David stopped him. He turned and burst out, "Look, bud. I don't want anything to do with your religion! All that stuff is a bunch of crap! If God cares about me, why doesn't He show Himself to me?" He pointed his finger in David's face. "I don't want to hear about it!"

David stayed calm. "Michael, you can't deny that there is more to this life than what we see here on earth. How would you explain what happened to my leg the other day if God didn't miraculously heal it?"

Michael's jaw stuck out. "I don't know and I don't care. But just because I don't have an answer doesn't mean your answer is correct."

"Maybe not, but it makes a lot more sense than any other explanation. Michael, God is showing Himself to you every day. You just haven't looked for Him. I'm telling you again. I do not spite you for anything, and I am not out to get you. I'm here to help you, and I will continue doing so no matter what you do. Michael…" David paused to get his attention. "God loves you." With that he turned and walked away, praying that God would do a work in Michael's hurting heart.

Michael stared after him for a long time before moving. He had never met anyone like David. This guy confused him, but he was not about to accept David's faith. No, let David Pearl be the nice guy, but it wouldn't get him anywhere. Michael smirked.

9

LOST!

David sat motionless with his back against the trunk of an ancient, moss-covered oak tree. He had heard some dry leaves rustle and a small twig break off to his right. Hardly daring to breathe, he kept his head completely still and taxed his peripheral vision, trying to see what was coming through the forest. Slowly, a tawny figure came into view, followed by what seemed to be a small shadow. As they haltingly moved into David's vision, he could see that it was a female deer and her newborn fawn. Suddenly, the doe stopped. David knew she had caught sight of his figure and was nervous about him. He was not in camouflage so she could easily see him. However, a slight wind was blowing toward David, so he knew she couldn't smell him. Still, she was skittish. David didn't move a muscle. He could see the fawn peering under its mother's belly with curious eyes. He didn't seem to be bothered with David, supposing him to be part of the woodland scenery. Instead, the fawn was more interested with the tip of a fern that tickled his nose when he sniffed it. Suddenly he sneezed. The mother deer jumped. David tried hard not to laugh. Gradually, the duo ambled off into the woods and were lost among the woodland giants.

David loved the flora and fauna of God's creation. He had only been sitting by the tree about fifteen minutes when the deer came through. It was Friday evening at the Dunamis retreat, and the students had been sent out to spend some quiet reflective time in God's presence. David had decided to find a solitary spot in the woods with his Bible and diary. However, it didn't seem very solitary as David heard yet another rustle in the woods. This time it was not as stealthy. Into view strode one of the students from a different college. It was Joey; David had met him earlier. Seeing David, Joey stopped and then turned and walked toward him.

"I know we're supposed to be alone out here," he said, "but since I accidentally bumped into you, I know God wants me to tell you this now. Earlier when we were praying together as a group, God asked me to tell you something, and I wanted to wait until we were alone. I don't know why I'm to do this or how it applies to you…but here goes. These are the words God gave me for you: 'I have a job for you. When it comes time you will know it. Until then, just wait. But when it comes, don't hesitate. Don't hesitate. David…*don't hesitate!*"

Joey stopped and looked straight at him. David returned his gaze for a moment before speaking. "Joey, I appreciate your obedience to step out in faith and share that with me. Thanks a lot! I don't know what it means either, but I'm sure I will soon. Thanks again."

Joey pursed his lips in an understanding grin and gave a slight nod. "No problem. I'll see you later." Just before he stepped out of sight, Joey glanced back in time to see David pick up his diary and start writing.

————◆————

Dusk began to fall. David picked himself up and dusted off the seat of his pants. He felt content and peaceful after having spent some time in the presence of the sovereign Lord. With a song in his heart and a bounce in his step, he made his way back to the trail that led to the cabins. As he neared the lights, he knew he would be one of the last students to straggle in from quiet time.

David entered the common fellowship hall and was immediately set upon by Donny. "Hey, dude!" he exclaimed. "Where've you been? You're just in time. C'mon! We're getting ready to play Telephone Pictionary!" Telephone Pictionary was a twist on the classic game of Pictionary. In it, a phrase or object was drawn and described alternately, and by the end of the round it looked nothing like what was originally written down. In essence, it was a written version of the children's game where a whispered phrase was passed down a line of people and ended up totally different from the original statement.

"I don't know…" hesitated David.

"Oh, don't give me that, you big party pooper! Get yourself in here!" And with that, Donny pulled his roommate into the circle of already seated students. Everyone laughed as David pretended to protest to an unrelenting Donny. "Now, now! None of that!" he tut-tutted with his finger wagging in David's face.

David gave in. "Okay, Donny. I'll play…under one condition. You get up to go running with me tomorrow morning. It's about time for you to get some good aerobic exercise." More laughter ensued as Donny's face drooped. Everyone knew that David had been trying to get Donny on a run for a long time.

"C'mon, you big party pooper!" wheedled David.

With everyone watching and ribbing him, Donny didn't have much of a choice, and he relented. "All right, we'll go running. But I'm warning you, you might have to carry me back!"

David just laughed. He looked around the room. "Where's Andrea?"

Somebody piped up from across the circle, "We're not sure. We haven't seen her since everyone left for quiet time. She's the only one out yet. She'll come in soon."

The game started and all was quiet for a while as the students wrote words and phrases down and drew the ones that they received from their neighbor. Then as the pictures were laid out next to the description of what they were supposed to be, raucous laughter rose in an uneven crescendo. Few were accurate depictions of the original description.

———————

Unnoticed by all but Donny, David rose and slipped out of the room. A few minutes passed and he did not return. Donny stood and said, "Hey, guys, I'll be right back."

Stepping outside he found David leaning against the porch railing and peering out into the starlit darkness. Without turning his head, David murmured, "I'm worried, Donny. It's not like her to stay out after dark like this, especially in unfamiliar territory."

Donny responded in a reassuring tone, "I'm sure she's fine. In fact, she's probably in her bunkhouse right now."

"I already checked and she's not there." Several moments passed in silence. Then David spoke up, "I'm going out to find her."

"Wait," said Donny. "We're coming with you. A lot of us can search better than one person alone."

David thought about arguing because he did not want to upset anyone, but he knew Donnie was right. "Okay, go get them."

Fifteen people gathered on the porch, including Rebecca, Cathy, and Derek. "Listen up," declared David.

"Andrea hasn't been seen since the start of quiet time. She would never stay out this late alone unless something was wrong. Travel in groups of two and three and don't wander off alone. Everyone keep their cell phone with them in case we need to contact each other. Don't go deep into the forest, at least not yet. Just check a small distance off each side of the trails. I don't think Andrea would wander too far off of them."

John piped up, "Maybe Andrea has her phone. Why don't we just call her?"

"I already tried that," responded David. "That's partly what has me worried. I'm hoping that she just left it on vibrate with her stuff in the cabin. Let's pray together and then get out there and find her!"

Everyone gathered in a circle and joined hands as David led them in prayer. "Dear Heavenly Father, we gather here as Your children with a request. Lord, You know where Andrea is and we're asking that You show us now. You promise us in Your Word that where two or three are gathered in Your name that You are there. Well, we have far more than two or three here, and God, we know that You hear us. Protect her, keep her safe and guide us to her quickly. Thank You, Jesus!" They stood quietly for a quick moment of silence.

"Okay, let's head out. It's eight thirty now. Meet back here by nine thirty so that we can regroup if we need to. But that's not going to happen." Rebecca looked at

David closely in the dim light and could see his jaw tense and his fists clench in determination. She was scared for her best friend and understood the worry that was going through David. Still, she admired him for taking charge like he did.

As they moved off, Rebecca teamed up with Donny and Derek while David and Cathy took the other side of the path. To extend their range most effectively, these two groups stayed within earshot of each other. They slowly combed each side of the path with their flashlights. Apart from the noises of the search parties and Andrea's name being shouted now and again, all was still and silent. Almost too silent. Everything had an eerie glow around it due to the silver strip of moonlight shining down through the night. David lost all track of time as he continually prayed for Andrea. At one point, Cathy broke down and began crying. David stopped to put a comforting arm around her shoulders. "It's alright, Cathy. We'll find her. Remember that God is in control, and He knows exactly where she is."

Cathy wiped at her eyes. "I know. It's just that Andrea has helped me with so much lately. She's been such an encouragement to me. We *have* to find her!"

"We will," promised David. "But I need you to stay strong and dry up those tears so you can actually see!" They moved off again.

Suddenly, a figure loomed up to one side of them. It was Donny. "David! Cathy! Get over here, quick! We found her!"

They hurried after him as he made his way back to the trail and crossed over to the other side. David was plying him with questions. "Hey! How did you find her? Is she all right? Speak up, man! Is she okay?"

All Donny would say is, "I don't know. Just get over here fast! She was lying still when we found her. I don't know if she was unconscious or what, but I hurried off to find you so I don't really know."

They finally reached the others. Derek was standing to one side, and Rebecca was sitting cross-legged on the ground with Andrea's head cradled on her lap. She was quietly sobbing and saying, "Wake up, Andi! Wake up! What's wrong?"

David was in shock. He looked at Derek. "She's not… she's not…" His voice trailed off. Derek shook his head. "Rebecca and I found a pulse, but she's not waking up. We don't know what's wrong."

David knelt down and felt the beating pulse for himself. Her stomach and chest were moving slowly up and down in rhythmic breathing, and nothing seemed wrong. She just looked like she was sleeping. David did not understand it. He took one of Andrea's hands in his and in a steady voice said, "Andrea, wake up. Andrea, come back to us. We need you, Andi." Nothing happened. A little louder this time, David said, "Andrea! Andrea!" He paused. He had felt something more than he had seen it. Peering closer, he saw her eyelids flutter then blink open all at once. David lowered his forehead to Andrea's hand as he gave the Lord a quick prayer of thanks. Then he stood up and stepped back.

"What's going on?" asked Andrea. "What's…? Why is it dark? Where are we?"

Rebecca took charge. "Just hold on, Andi. Do you feel all right? Does anything hurt?"

Andrea shook her head in confusion. "No. Why do you think something's wrong." She sat up and began trying to stand.

Donny jumped over and gave her a hand. "Careful, Andrea. Are you sure you're okay?"

"Yeah. I feel great! The only thing is that I'm a bit chilly. But what's going on here, people?"

Donny, Derek, Cathy, Rebecca, and David all looked at each other and broke out in huge grins of relief. "Oh, Andrea! We were so worried about you," said Cathy. "Let's get you back to camp and we'll tell you."

David handed his jacket to Andrea. "Here, Andi, this'll keep you warm 'til we get back."

She smiled sweetly. "Thanks, Dave."

———————— ❍ ————————

Back at camp, Andrea bundled herself in a blanket and took a seat by the campfire. David's jacket had been returned and the other search parties had been called in. Everyone gathered around as the story was compiled.

"First off," started Rebecca, "you know you've been out there in the woods since the start of quiet time?"

Andrea lifted her eyebrows. "I guessed that I must have been, but I don't understand how it could've been so long. All I did was doze off and dream a quick dream. I don't see how it could have been several hours."

Sitting in the darkness, David's eyebrows bunched. Andrea seemed too nonchalant. And what was this dream? Before he could say anything, Cathy asked, "A quick dream? What was the dream about?"

Andrea shrugged her shoulders. "It wasn't a big deal. I've never understood how dreams work. They're so real and yet they're so unreal. Like in this case, I thought it was a quick dream, but it must have taken a lot longer than I thought. Sorry to scare you all. I don't even remember dozing off. I didn't mean to create such a stir." David now knew that Andrea was hiding something; she had not answered the question about the dream.

Derek spoke up, "It's okay. We're just so relieved that we found you and that you're okay. We didn't know what had happened. By the way," he added, "did you have your cell phone on you, or did you leave it at your cabin?"

"I left it with my stuff in the cabin. Why?"

"Because that's what partly had us so worried. We tried your cell and when you didn't answer, we hoped that you had left it behind."

"Sorry again, guys," said Andrea. "I feel really bad about this."

"Well don't," stated Rebecca emphatically as she came over to give her friend a big hug. "We're just glad you're back safe and sound, so don't go and ruin it for yourself. Hey! I have an idea. Let's all sing some songs of thanksgiving to God right here around the fire. John! Go grab your guitar. We'll wait for you."

A few minutes later, the strumming of the guitar, the melody of the raised voices, and the spiral of smoke from the campfire rose up to heaven as the stars twinkled back in an astronomic salute.

10

The Dream

David's sleep was restless, yet when he awoke in the morning he felt somehow refreshed. It was still early and no one else was up yet, but that was how he liked it when he went running in the morning. Quietly he slipped into his clothes and made his way over to Donny's bunk. He laughed silently at his friend snoring away with his mouth open and his sheets scattered every which way. Gently he shook him by the shoulder. Donnie snorted a couple times and swallowed. "Wha' 'assat for?"

"Come on, buddy! Time for you to get yourself up and go runnin' with me."

Donny rolled over and grunted. "Sorry, Dave. Sometime I will, but not today."

"Oh no, you don't!" responded David. "Do I need to get some water for your ear? It looks thirsty."

Donny sat straight up in bed. "Nope. It's quite hydrated this morning, thank you very much. Now about that jogging, I think I might just have to give that a try this morning. Where's my shoes?"

David laughed as he tossed his friend's footgear at him. "Here ya go. Meet me outside."

A few minutes later, Donny stumbled outside, still rubbing at the sleepers in his eyes. "Are you sure you want to do this, you bloomin' antelope?"

"Absolutely! I wouldn't miss this for the world, you great lumbering tortoise you!"

"The world you say? I'll take the world, thank you very much! And you can be lucky I'm not a tortoise or I'd hide in my shell and nothing you could do would ever get me out to go running. Ha! You wouldn't be able to pour water in my ear then!"

David smiled. "Save your breath. I'm sure you'll need every bit you can get in just a few minutes. Come on, let's get going."

Together, the two friends loped away on one of the many woodland trails that encircled the camp.

Half an hour later, Andrea, Rebecca, and Cathy were in the middle of a vast field, picking wildflowers. Wild poppies, violets, and daffodils were in abundance. They laughed and joked together, taking pictures of each other among the flowers in the morning sunlight.

Across the field, David and Donny walked out of the woods. They had been jogging for a while and were walking for a bit to catch their breaths. Donny was especially winded. David caught sight of the girls across the field and pointed, saying, "Hey! I'll race you to the girls!"

Donny held up a hand as he shook his head. "Huh-uh. No way. I'm already out of breath. There's no question who would win."

David begged to differ. "You've always been better at sprints than me. I'm cut out for long distance running. You might have a chance. I'll even let you wait a bit to catch your breath."

Donny looked doubtful, but finally he relented. After a few minutes, he felt ready to go. Both boys got down in a ready position. David slowly said, "Ready…set…*go!*"

Donny shot off as fast as he could with David trailing slightly but holding his own. Cathy had heard David shout the word *go* and laughed out loud. "Hey, Andrea, Rebecca! Look at this."

Donny was pumping the air furiously with both arms, his legs working like pistons as he tried to go faster. David had a huge grin plastered over his face like a little kid running away from his mother. Cathy raised her hands on each side to act as the finish line. Whoever hit her hand first would be the winner.

Donny was still in the lead, but not by much. Closer and closer they came, with David closing the gap bit by bit. With only fifteen yards to spare, he took advantage of his longer legs and, with a quick burst of speed, flew past Donny. In one fluid movement, David threw himself into a forward handspring and slapped Cathy's hand as he came up. Andrea and Rebecca cheered as Donny skidded to a halt with a comical look on his face. "What? That's no fair! You cheater you! You're nothin' but a big showoff, that's it!"

David raised an eyebrow. "Cheater? How'd I cheat?"

"You…you…ran…faster. You're not allowed to do that." He went into a pretend pout.

Andrea threw an arm around Donny's shoulders. "It's okay. What you didn't know is that the winner has to carry the loser back to camp on his shoulders."

Donny perked up and turned to David. "I say, old bean, did you hear that? What a super wheeze! That girl's got as much brains as she's got beauty, let me tell you!"

David was standing in bewilderment. "What the…? Andrea, what're you doing? Don't encourage the blighter. He's already got me all tuckered out!"

The girls were laughing hysterically at the triumphant look on Donny's face as he chased David around trying to get on his back. David pretended to run away but finally gave in. "All right, buster. I wish you hadn't taken your pester pill this morning."

"Pester pill, nothing," responded Donny. "This is just me. Simple, undiluted Donny Fresnett!"

David knelt down as Donny threw his legs around his neck and took a seat on his shoulders. "Hah! Then I wouldn't want to know what you're like after taking a pester pill! Augh! Quit choking me! Get your legs under my arms and let me hold them. Don't wrap them around my esophagus, boulder bottom!"

"Boulder bottom yourself, wobbly legs. C'mon, stand up! Up, I say! We're getting nowhere!"

"Oof. For as skinny as you look, you sure have some body weight to you. All right, here we go."

Donny rubbed his hands together in anticipation. "Ooh goodie. I wonder what it's like to be as tall as you. This oughta be...*whoa!*" David had stood up suddenly, and Donny almost lost his balance and fell off his shoulders. "Easy does it, big guy. You're not a rocket. You don't have to shoot up so fast. Be more like an elevator...nice and easy. Think elevator."

"Elevator indeed," David snorted as he struggled to keep his balance. "Just be glad you didn't win. You would've had to carry me on your shoulders! All right girls"—he turned around to face them—"I think we're ready."

All three were lying among the flowers, holding their sides and wiping at the tears that were flowing down their cheeks. Laughter bubbled out of them like water out of springs at the antics of their two friends. Donny looked down his nose at them in mock disdain. "Look at them!

Impudent females! What do they think they're hooting on about? Daft as ducks if ya ask me."

David did his best to shake his head but had a hard time with Donny's knees clamping tight on each side. "Well, no one asked you, my friend, but I don't understand it either. Can't imagine what could be so funny." He twisted around in each direction. "Nope, I can't see anything around here that would make me laugh that hard, can you, matey?"

Donny shaded his eyes with a hand as he looked toward the horizon. "Nope, it's got me confounded. Ah well, let the beauties go on with their chortling and chuckling and cackling. C'mon let's go. They'll catch us soon at the rate you're going, you lumbering ox! C'mon pick it up! Giddyup!"

Struggling to rise, the girls stumbled after the guys, still laughing at the constant string of friendly banter flying up and down between the two friends.

Later that day, after worship and a message from the guest speaker, David found a slip of paper being pressed into his hand. It came from Andrea as she passed by him. She didn't look at him, and it was obvious that she didn't want anyone to know what she had done. David pocketed it and discreetly looked around. No one seemed to have noticed. A few minutes later, Andrea, who was now seated on the other side of the room, saw David get up and leave. She knew he was leaving in order to read her message.

Dear Dave,

> *I want to talk to you. Meet me at 2:30 today at the spot where you guys found me last night. Thanks so much!*

Andi

Lunch passed and the afternoon slowly dragged on. The girls had gathered to do something on their own, and the guys were in the middle of an Ultimate Frisbee match. As two thirty drew near, David excused himself. Donny was curious. "What's up, bud? Usually you can't break away from physical activity like this!"

David shrugged it off. "Not much. I just want to spend some time away from all the noise." He gave his friend a look that Donny knew well. It meant he was not supposed to ask questions.

Donny nodded. "Okay, let me know if you need anything. I'm here for ya."

"Thanks. I appreciate it."

As David approached the location, he could see Andrea sitting on a fallen log. Her hair seemed even more golden in the ray of sunlight that fell on her as it passed through the leaves on the trees. Mentally, he thanked God for his friendship with Andrea and asked for strength to keep this conversation pure.

Andrea smiled at him as he entered the glade. "Welcome!" she said. "No one knows you came, do they?"

David shook his head. "No. Donny was curious, but he doesn't know where I went."

"Okay. It wouldn't have been a big deal if someone knew, but I just wanted to share this with you."

"All right, so let's hear about your dream." David took a seat next to her on the log.

Andrea chuckled. "I figured you knew what this was about, which is why I wanted to talk to you alone today. I knew you weren't satisfied with my explanation last night."

"How did you know?"

"I told you a few weeks ago that you'd be surprised what females can pick up in guys."

"All right, I guess I'll have to take that as an answer. So let's hear it."

Andrea took a deep breath before beginning. "Well, yesterday I had an amazing quiet time. There was no music playing, there was no preaching, but right here in this very spot, God's presence was so real to me…it was incredible. I felt my spirit get lighter and stronger. It was just…just… man! I can't even describe it! All I know is that God was really strengthening me for some reason."

David made a comment, "Generally, that means that He's getting you ready for some hardship or trial. But anyhow, continue."

"Well, I can hardly say that I fell asleep yesterday. It was more like God put me to sleep. And I didn't have a dream—it was more of a vision. I can't explain it any other way. As I was sitting there"—she paused and pointed to a mossy spot on the ground—"I was praying and worshipping God, and even though my eyes were closed, it was almost like I could see. It was like my body had become lighter and I was rising up through the clouds. Eventually, I couldn't see the earth anymore. Suddenly, I had the feeling that I was in something like a huge palace, but at the same time I knew I was still in the sky. Everything was dark and I couldn't see anything. Then I felt a hand take mine. I didn't know anyone was there, but I wasn't startled at all when He touched me. How do I know it was a male? I don't know how I knew—I just did.

"As soon as He took my hand, I saw a light in the distance, but almost like it was coming from around a corner. I began to move toward it, and my Companion came with me. It was a long way, but as we walked, He kept talking to me. I can't remember anything that He told me, but I remember that the more He talked to me, the happier and fuller and lighter and more joyful I became. Finally we came to the corner. The light was very bright now, and I stopped. I suddenly had the feeling that if I stepped around that corner, I would die. I knew that that light was coming straight from God.

"My Companion reassured me saying, 'Do not fear, Andrea. God has brought you here for a reason. You must see what is around the corner.'

"I still thought I was going to die, but I forced myself to take a step into the direct light. By some miracle, my eyes were able to handle the light, and I could see that it was shining from the most beautiful throne that you could ever imagine. I'm not even going to try to explain it because it would be impossible. At that moment, I fell down like the apostle John in the book of Revelation where it says that he became like a dead person. But my Companion placed His right hand on me and said, 'Look again.'

"I raised my head and saw a man at the foot of the throne. He was dancing with all the strength in his body. His face was obscured to me. I couldn't see it clearly. I still don't know who it was. But even though I couldn't see his face, I could feel the joy flowing out of him. And all I wanted to do was to run and dance with him before the King of kings and Lord of lords. My Companion somehow knew this and restrained me saying, 'You can't go, Andrea, not yet. You're still needed on earth.'

"I tried to pull away and run to the foot of the throne, but I heard Him say again, 'Andrea, Andrea!' And it was at that moment that I woke up. The vision seemed like it took fifteen minutes, but I must have been laying there for hours."

Andrea stopped and stared at the ground. "I can still see and feel everything. I want to forget everything here and go back and dance for joy with that man in the presence of the Lord. What do you think it means?"

David did not answer for a moment. Finally he spoke, "I have no clue, Andi. All I know is that God wants you to remember the joy you felt when you stood in His presence. Remember that when you hit the tidal waves of hardship that will certainly come. I don't know what your dream is supposed to mean, but you'll understand it when the time is right. He wanted you to have that experience for a reason, and He'll show you what it means." David smiled at Andrea. "Thanks for sharing that with me."

11

The Cloud

Back at Pinevale, campus life was dead. Many students had left for the weekend, so the sidewalks and buildings were nearly deserted, although several dining units were kept open, including The Kitchen in the Lodge.

Jason Portello was bored. He was also lonely; he had no close friends at college. David was probably his closest friend, but he didn't even know David that well. Besides, he was away for the weekend on that spring retreat. *Oh well,* thought Jason. *I guess I might as well get a bite to eat and then turn in early.*

Motoring his way to The Kitchen, Jason passed by the steps that led up to the main entrance of the Lodge in order to reach the ramp that provided him access to the front doors. Slowly, he spun his wheelchair 180 degrees and started up the ramp. As soon as he did, he knew that he had picked the wrong time to come to the Lodge, because at the top of the ramp was none other than Michael Dervin with that twisted sneer that Jason had come to know and hate. Deciding to act strong, he pushed the lever on his chair forward and continued up the ramp. Michael waited for him to approach and stood squarely in his path so that he couldn't get around him. "Well, well, well, if it isn't the crybaby, Mr. 'Leave-me-alone' himself!" taunted Michael.

Jason tried to do what he had seen David do and looked Michael straight in the eyes. "Let me pass," he said tersely.

Michael feigned surprise. "Don't get *pushy*." And as he said the word *pushy*, he placed his foot on the front of the wheelchair and gave it a mighty shove.

The wheelchair skidded backward and slammed into the railing alongside the ramp. Jason's head jerked as he came to a stop. He decided to try a little of Michael's own medicine on him. "Why don't you pick on someone your own size? Oh, but that's right, you're too scared to do that. I heard you turned and ran after you tried to pick on a guy with crutches and all of a sudden he started walking without them."

Michael's face turned red with livid anger. He began kicking and jamming the wheelchair against the rail again and again as he yelled, "You wouldn't know the true story because you weren't there, idiot! It seems to me that you had already turned tail and run! Don't you *ever* say that I'm scared of anyone! Y'hear me? Never again! *Never again!*"

Michael cooled down enough to keep his voice composed, but he continued with his mocking, "How do you like it when your hero David Pearl isn't around to step in and take care of the situation for you, huh? He's not going to get in my way this time! Ha! He's far away at that religious camp. By the way, church boy, why aren't you there with all your other Jesus-freak friends?"

Jason tried to defend himself and at least make himself look a bit better in Michael's eyes. "I'm not a church boy... and I'm not part of that Christian group."

Michael just laughed at him. "Well, you're always hanging out with David, and he's a church boy. Ha! Not going on that retreat was just about the only good thing you've done all year! You're not good for anything. You just get in everybody's way, like right now!" Michael gave the wheelchair one last shove as he stomped past Jason and continued down the ramp. Jason sat for a long time in silence, tears running down his cheeks, his wheelchair jammed against the railing. Time stopped as those last words flowed unbidden through his mind like ghosts haunting his thoughts, echoing, reverberating, multiplying. They kept returning louder and louder. "You're not good for anything! You've only done one good thing all year! You just get in everybody's way! You're not good for anything!"

Straining to see through a veil of tears, Jason turned his wheelchair around and headed down the ramp toward his dorm as fast as his chair would go.

Jason went hungry that night.

At that very moment, the group at the spring retreat had just finished eating and were settling down for a time of worship and prayer. Instruments were tuned and for half an hour they worshipped and glorified God. Afterward, the students broke up into small groups and spent some time in prayer for each other and for specific prayer requests. When asked if he had anything that he wanted prayer for, David responded, "Actually there is something. Pray for Jason and Michael, two students that I met at college this year. Jason has been confined to a wheelchair his whole life and Michael has decided to make him his whipping boy. He's always bullying Jason and making fun of him because of his handicap. Pray that Michael would see the pain he is causing and that Jason would find the grace to forgive him."

The group bowed their heads and lifted these two students up to the throne of God.

Jason had not slept. Even now the sun was peeping through the window blinds, and he felt as if he had only dozed for about ten minutes the whole night. His confrontation with Michael played relentlessly through his head. Over and over again, he saw himself as weak, helpless, and entirely unable to defend himself. Over and over again, Michael's words played through his head, words that he had grown accustomed to hearing throughout his life. Not everyone had verbally expressed them, but most had treated him that way. *You're not good for anything! You've only done one good thing all year! You just get in everybody's way!*

Slowly, over the sleepless night, an evil idea had entered Jason's mind. It was a very small, disturbing thought when it first presented itself, but large enough to be noticed. At first, Jason had cast it aside as absurd, but the more he thought about it, the more he considered it as a possibility. And so the idea grew larger.

He weighed the ramifications of acting upon such an idea. He had never pictured himself as capable of doing something like this. He tried to think about other things, but his mind harbored ill thoughts toward everyone. *Nobody cares about me. Well...maybe David does a little, but that's it. Life seems to be pointless. I'm getting nowhere and everybody finds enjoyment in making my life more miserable. God doesn't even care about me. David says He does, but if God really cared, He'd do something about my situation. He healed David, but He won't heal me.* The idea grew larger.

Jason turned all his attention to this new thought. *I don't like what will happen to me if I do this, but it will be better to stay somewhere in peace for the rest of my life than be harassed by everyone around me.* He then closed his eyes to steel his nerves. Unseen by him, a thick cloud slid silently across the sun, darkening everything below it. The idea no longer grew; it had reached maturity.

That same morning, David had taken another run, only this time without Donny. When he returned to camp, he realized that everyone was still in bed. That didn't surprise him, as he liked to get up earlier than most. Rather than disturb the slumbering students, he decided to spend some time alone with God. Walking down to the lake, David strolled out onto the large wooden dock that extended fifty feet into the lake. A nostalgic feeling came over him as he crossed his arms and rested them on the top of one of the large wooden pillars that extended above the walkway of the dock. He rested his chin on his arms and gazed out across the lake. The rays of the sun wafted over him like the blast of a slow-heating oven. He loved times like this when he could revel in the presence and the creation of Almighty God. He closed his eyes as he basked in the warmth of the sun and the presence of the Son. For all the warmth, he felt a chill run down his spine.

Suddenly, he felt rather than heard someone nearby him. He opened his eyes and looked over to see Andrea leaning on the adjacent pillar. She too was gazing in silent admiration at the beauty before them: the dancing wavelets adorned with dazzling crystals of light that skipped to and fro, the golden rays of the sun, the sun-kissed hills on the other side of the lake covered in the rainbow of colors that can be seen on a beautiful spring morning. Everything was at peace.

"How long ago did you get here?" murmured David.

"Just now."

They stood in silence. Neither of them wanted to forget this moment of perfection in nature.

"It's gorgeous." breathed Andrea. "Simply breathtaking!"

"We are blessed, Andi."

"I know."

"Andi…"

Andrea knew that tone of voice. It meant that David was thinking and that he was about to share some spiritual encouragement or something that God had showed him. Previously, she might have been turned off at his constant emphasis on the things of God, but she had grown to appreciate it. She respected David's wisdom and listened so she could learn as much as possible. She also knew that in this pristine setting, he would probably be even more contemplative than usual.

"Yes?"

"Andrea…I…" He paused.

She looked at him. "Yes?" Silence. "C'mon, buddy, just spit it out. I'm all ears."

"Andi, no matter what happens in life, I want you to promise me several things."

Bemused, she nodded. "Okay."

"I want you to promise me that you'll always trust in God. I want you to promise that you'll always remember that no matter what happens in life, He is still in control,

He still loves you, and He still has a perfect plan that cannot be hindered by anything. I want you to promise that you'll expend your life for the gospel and that you'll press on and live for Jesus no matter what happens to discourage you or tear you down. I want you to promise me these things."

Andrea looked quizzically at her friend. He was still staring out across the lake. It puzzled her that he said these things now. She stood silently as she pondered all that he had just asked of her. She did not intend to make promises she could not keep, but after thinking about it for a minute, she knew that deep down inside this is what she wanted anyway. "David…" She waited until he looked at her and held his gaze for a moment. "I promise." She studied his eyes; they mirrored their surroundings. Peacefulness shone from them in absolute clarity.

David smiled in affirmation and turned to gaze across the lake again. Without warning, a large dark cloud sailed out of nowhere and moved across the face of the sun. David felt a second shiver run the length of his spine, but this was not like the shiver he had experienced a few minutes earlier. Andrea saw David's whole body stiffen. From the side, she could see his eyes squint together a little.

"David? What is it?" Andrea asked.

No reply. He continued staring straight before him without moving. It almost looked like he was listening. Andrea stood quietly, not wanting to disturb him. She did not sense anything and wondered what had gotten into

David, but she also knew he would never ignore her unless he had a good reason to.

Finally, he spoke, "Andrea, I can't tell you right now. I need you to do me a favor and not ask any questions. All I can tell you is that I know who the man in your dream was. Remember the one you said was dancing before the throne of God? I know who it was, but I can't tell you right now. Please understand." He turned to look at her.

Andrea stifled a gasp, and her body swayed backward slightly before she composed herself. In the space of about a minute, David's eyes had completely changed. Again, Andrea found herself wondering at the depth and fullness of his eyes. It was as if they had a life of their own! A moment ago, they had spoken peace. Now there seemed to be a multitude of emotions swirling around in them. She had never before known his eyes to be so complex. Usually, she could sense one or two emotions in them when she looked at them. Now they were confusing; it scared her, and she lowered her gaze.

David realized Andrea's bewilderment and turned again to face the lake. Andrea quickly prayed for understanding and began to feel a renewed strength and comfort. She closed her eyes. "David," she began, "I don't know what just happened. But something just changed within you. I could see it in your eyes. One moment you were happy and peaceful, and the next you were…I don't know what. I will honor your request. I won't ask you any questions.

Whatever God has revealed to you, He revealed it for a reason, and He will reveal it to me in His time. But now I need you to do me a favor and remember those promises that you just had me make. You need to step back from whatever you just saw or heard or felt and understand that it's okay. God's in control. You need to rest in His care and not be worried. Don't be distressed! Don't let this…this… thing, or whatever it is…ruin this beautiful day." Andrea kept her eyes tight shut.

Moments passed. A duck quacked in the reeds along the side of the lake. A light breeze played with Andrea's hair and made David's stick up arrogantly. "Andrea…" David's voice came smoothly and surely. "Andrea, look at me." Andrea did not want to face those eyes again, but she slowly turned to face him. "Thank you, Andrea! Thank you so much!" David's voice rose in sincerity. "I really needed to hear that. I'm sorry I let it overcome me like that. Please forgive me."

Looking into his eyes, all Andrea could see was softness, tenderness, pure sincerity, and once again, peace. In that instant, her heart just about burst with joy. She smiled, and rarely had David seen such a big smile from her. Her cheeks dimpled, and her hair glittered in the sun. "No problem, Dave. There is nothing to forgive. It's all good."

Just then, a shout interrupted her. They turned to see Donny gesturing at them from the top of the hill. "You two better hurry up if ya want any breakfast! I'm starvin', and if you don't get up here fast, there might not be any flapjacks left!"

David grinned at Andrea. "We better go or old famine face won't leave anything for his two poor friends."

Laughing, they started climbing the hill under Donny's indignant response. "I heard that!"

12

"Don't Hesitate!"

David sat at his desk, scribbling away in his diary. It was ten o' clock the following Monday. Donny struggled into the dorm room under a bulging backpack. "Yo, dude!" he said. "You know what? It stinks coming back to schoolwork and classes after such a great weekend, especially if you have to get up early like I did for an eight o'clock class! You're a lucky bum, that's what you are."

David simply grunted.

Donald cocked his head and studied David's turned back for a moment. "Hey, bud, you okay? Ever since the end of the retreat, you've been kinda morose, if I may say so. Something is wrong. What is it?"

David's shoulder's bounced up and down in a quick shrug, and Donny could hear his pen continue to slide across the page. Donny became curious. He crossed the room to stand behind David and asked, "Whatcha writin'?"

David's journal slammed shut with a bang and Donny jumped. "I'm sorry," said David. "I can't let you see."

Donny looked him in the eyes. There was no hint of joking or mischievousness on his friend's face. He couldn't believe it. "Okay, something is seriously wrong with you, Dave. Never...and I mean *never* have you refused to let me see your entries."

Slowly, David stood and placed his hands on his best friend's shoulders. "I'm sorry, Donny. I wish I could show you, and sometime you will see it, but not right now. This entry would do nothing but harm if you were to see it now. Please trust me!" David dropped his hands.

After a moment of silence, Donny sighed. "All right, Dave. I won't take this personally. But I don't like how you're acting. Something is majorly wrong, and I don't like not being able to share your burden and help you out."

David managed a weak grin. "I understand. Thanks. I do appreciate you, Donny. You have been an immense help and support. But if you want to help, then pray. Pray hard. I need it more than I ever have before. But I must carry this on my own, no one can share it. I wish it didn't have to be this way, I'd like to tell you, but I can't. Please pray, Donny!"

Donny nodded. "Sure thing, bro! Now cheer up! At least for my sake!"

David smiled. "Sorry. I'll try, but I need to keep writing. Don't let me bother you. Go find something to keep occupied with. Sorry, Donny."

Three hours later, David had finished writing, eaten lunch, and was walking down the sidewalk to his statistics class. As usual, he left early so he did not have to rush. Suddenly, he caught sight of Michael Dervin in front of him, and he ran to catch up. "Hi, Michael! Where are you off to?"

Michael saw him and rolled his eyes. "You again? Why don't you just bug off?"

"Because I'm walking in the same direction as you, and I already told you I care for you and I'm going to be your friend whether you're mine or not." David saw Michael's jaw clench. "So you never answered my question. Where are you off to?"

"It doesn't matter. But I wish it was somewhere else."

"Why is that?"

"Because it's obviously in the same direction that you're heading."

David actually laughed. "Michael, I'm sorry. That just struck me as funny. You're cracking me up with the lengths that you're taking to be rude. Don't mind me. Hey! That's Jason up there in his wheelchair." David stopped Michael and faced him. "Listen, friend, I don't want problems here, so don't say anything to Jason to stir things up, okay?"

Michael didn't have much choice. David was there. As they approached, Jason looked back and saw who was coming. He pulled over to one side of the sidewalk. Michael walked by with his nose in the air, but David greeted him.

"Hey, man! How's it going? Are you headed to class?" David nodded at the backpack that Jason held on his lap.

"No, I just got out of class. I'm headed back to my place."

"Oh, okay. Lucky you! I'm just starting a class now. Oh well. Hey! We need to catch up! I'll talk to you soon!"

"See ya."

"Later. Hey, Michael, wait up!" Michael had continued walking, and David jogged a short distance before catching him. "Thanks for not saying anything, Michael." Just then a thought hit him. "Hey! Wait a minute…" He knew where Jason lived, and he was not headed in that direction. Why did he tell him that he was headed back to his dorm? David turned his head to look at Jason, and what he saw made his blood run cold.

———❧———

Jason couldn't believe it. Now David was even hanging out with Michael! *Well, I guess I've made the right decision.* Closing his eyes to steel himself, he slowly reached into his backpack. Suddenly, his eyes popped open and he stared at the two retreating figures. They were not twenty yards away. His hand came out with a death grip on the polished handle of his handgun. He raised it slowly and deliberately until it aligned with his line of sight—the unprotected back of Michael Dervin.

David froze. Two words flew through his mind. *Don't hesitate!* Without a second thought, David took a flying leap toward Michael, who had continued walking down the sidewalk. David crashed into him, sending him flying to the ground.

In that same instant, Michael experienced three things: an incredible rage at David, a pain in his ears from a terrible explosion, and…blackness. Everything went dark.

Andrea was in her dorm room on a break between classes. She had spent some time in prayer on her knees before God. This had become a daily habit in the past month; it always refreshed her and opened her heart to the Lord. Today, she couldn't get her mind off the conversation she had shared with David yesterday morning on the dock. She prayed about it and asked God to strengthen David. She didn't know what was wrong, but obviously something had really bothered him. She opened her Bible to 2 Samuel chapter 6 where yesterday she had been reading about King David. As she got to verse 14, it jumped off the page at her. She froze. It read, "And David was dancing before the Lord with all his might…"

After the gunshot, students on the sidewalk and the surrounding grounds froze. Some seemed incapable of moving, but others began diving to the ground or hiding behind trees. All they could see were two bodies on the ground surrounded by a pool of blood and a student in a wheelchair armed with a handgun. Screams rent the air. Panic spread like wildfire. Several students stayed calm enough to call 911, and sirens sounded as police cruisers sped toward the scene.

Andrea read the verse again. The Bible was speaking about King David, the second king of Israel, but now this verse had a personal meaning for Andrea. To her, it spoke clearly of David Pearl. She now knew, as David had known, who it was in her dream that had been dancing before the throne of God. It was him. It was him! Andrea looked up. "But why did God show me David dancing before Him in heaven when he's actually here on earth with me?"

Jason couldn't believe it. He was an expert at shooting pistols. When he pulled his gun out of the backpack, he did it just as he would on the shooting range. He took a deep breath, let half of it out, and held it. Both hands clasped the handle of the gun in front of him and, taking careful aim, he held the sights steadily in the middle of Michael's back. Nothing could go wrong. But as soon as he pulled the trigger, he knew something had gone terribly wrong. He didn't know how David had moved so fast, but somehow he knew he had shot the wrong person. Both Michael and David were lying motionless on the concrete, but he knew in his heart that he had just shot the one person who cared about him the most: David Pearl.

He had intended to shoot his enemy and then peacefully surrender to the police. He didn't care if he sat in jail his whole life. He had come to the end of his rope, and he was determined to do something about it. But now…this! Grief, guilt, anger, and frustration flowed over Jason. He couldn't take this. He slowly raised the gun to his own head and pulled the trigger.

――――▷●◁――――

Andrea's thoughts were suddenly interrupted. Sirens were going off all over campus. Almost immediately, her cell phone beeped four times, indicating a new text message. She checked it and read:

> *Attention all Pinevale students:*
>
> *This message has been sent from the university's emergency response system. There has been an emergency on the campus grounds, and we are asking that all students find shelter. If you are inside, stay there. Lock your doors and stay away from the windows. If outside,*

make your way to the nearest building and secure yourself. Stay calm and await further instructions. Thank you for your cooperation."

Andrea immediately followed the instructions on the message and locked her doors. Then she phoned David. No answer. That worried her, but she thought, *Maybe he's busy trying to find shelter. I wonder what's going on?* Next she tried Donny. It rang and rang. *C'mon, Donny! Pick up!*

Finally she heard his voice. "Hello?"

"Donny! This is Andrea. Do you know what's going on?"

"No, I have no clue. I just got the text message."

"Do you know where David is? I tried calling him and he didn't answer. I'm worried about him."

"Um, last I knew he was headed to his stats class. That was about ten minutes ago."

There was a short silence. "Donny?"

"Yeah?"

"Pray hard. I think this situation might have something to do with him."

"Why do you say that?"

"I'm not completely sure. Just pray. I'm going to keep trying his cell."

"Okay, see ya."

Andrea didn't even take the time to say good-bye. She immediately hung up and hit a speed dial button on her phone. She heard it ring four times, and then Andrea heard David's automated greeting. She hung up and dialed again.

Same thing. She dialed again. She didn't know why, but she thought if she called over and over he would finally answer. This time she was surprised to hear the phone answered, but her heart sank when she heard the voice. It was a female. She knew that it was not a good sign that someone other than David was answering his phone.

"Who is this?" she asked. There was a short silence on the other end before the woman started talking. Andrea cut her short and her voice began to rise in panic, "Is David all right? Where is he?" She could hear a loud siren in the background and knew that David's phone was at the scene of the emergency. "You're the police, aren't you?"

"Ma'am, who are you?" came the voice.

"I'm Andrea Hutchens. A close friend of David's."

"I'd like to talk to you. Are you a student at Pinevale?"

"Yes, I'm in 212 Elm Hall. You didn't answer my question. Where's David? Is he okay?"

The woman ignored her questions. "Stay right there, Miss Hutchens. I'm coming over to talk to you." The line clicked, and Andrea felt like a million pounds of pressure were pushing on her from every direction and that her body would implode at any moment.

Even though only minutes had passed, it seemed like an hour before there was a knock on her door. A glance through the peephole confirmed that it was an officer of the law. She opened the door. The policewoman took one look at Andrea's ashen face, and her heart went out to her. "You're Andrea?" Andrea nodded dumbly. "I'm

Trooper Alicia Davenport. I need to come in and ask you some questions."

They sat down and Andrea blurted out, "Where's David?"

Trooper Davenport held up a hand. "I know this is hard, but I need to ask you some questions first. To be honest, we rarely talk to students about incidents like this anyway, but since you kept calling David's cell phone, we thought you might know something about it."

About what? Tears began pushing out of Andrea's eyes and running down her cheeks. She knew in her spirit something was wrong, but she kept silent and waited for the trooper to continue.

"Do you know what David was doing twenty minutes ago?"

Andrea shook her head. "No, except his roommate just told me he had left a little bit ago for a class."

"Which class?"

"Statistics, I think."

"Do you know of any enemies that David had?"

"Enemies? No." She paused. "Ma'am, I know something is wrong and you're not making it any easier by just hinting at things."

"I understand that, Andrea. But I need your cooperation just a little longer. Do you understand? This is important. Try to be strong."

Andrea wiped at her eyes, sniffled, and nodded her head.

"Do the names Michael Dervin and Jason Portello mean anything to you?" Trooper Davenport watched her closely and could see the immediate recognition on her face.

"Yes, they do. Jason is confined to a wheelchair, and Michael has been bullying him for a while. David has intervened once or twice and has made friends with Jason. He's also reached out to Michael, but he hasn't been very successful with that relationship." She stopped.

The trooper had been scribbling in her notebook as Andrea talked, but when she said that Jason was David's friend, she paused and looked up at her. "You said that Jason and David were friends? Were they on good terms?"

Andrea nodded. Trooper Davenport looked puzzled but finished writing in her notebook. "Is there anything else you'd like to tell me?"

"No. I've told you all I know. Now it's your turn. Tell me the truth and don't hide anything from me, please."

Trooper Davenport sighed. "Andrea, what I'm going to tell you, you need to keep to yourself until we release this information. Do you understand?" After receiving affirmation, she continued, "I can't string this out, Andrea… your friend David is gone." Nothing else needed to be said; nothing else was important. Andrea simply sat and wept with tears flowing unchecked down her face. Trooper Davenport pulled Andrea close in a comforting hug. Andrea laid her head on her shoulder and squeezed her eyes shut, wanting to block everything out. Gone from her was the one she loved. Alicia Davenport simply held her as Andrea's tears darkened her uniform.

13

LIFE!

As the bullet thudded into David's body, he felt only a quick sting, like getting a shot at the doctor's office. The next instant, it was over. He almost expected more pain. Then he realized that he could see his body lying on the ground beside Michael. It was then that David understood that he no longer had a physical body. He could, however, see everything around him very clearly. He didn't have vision like he used to when he was physically alive, but somehow he was acutely aware of everything around him.

Suddenly, he felt a strong pull on his body. It felt like a huge electromagnet had fixed its power on him. He turned to look upward and from that point on, he never looked back toward the earth; he was too attracted to what was above. He couldn't see anything yet, but he knew that he was about to enter heaven.

The pull became stronger. It seemed to him that his spirit began to speed up, and the earth below him was quickly lost to view. Not that it mattered, because David was not in the least bit interested in going back. His current reality was such a higher state of being that David would not have gone back to his physical body if he'd had the choice. He suddenly became aware of a pinpoint of light above him that was growing larger. As he continued upward, he became aware of the absence of time. It shocked him. He tried to determine how long it had been since he had passed into this afterlife, but it seemed like two seconds and two years all at the same time. Then the thought occurred to him that he really could not even call this an afterlife. This *was* life. If anything, his experience on earth had only been a pre-life—life before real birth! This was it! This was *life*!

As David's spirit journey continued, he felt a stronger and stronger sense of everything around him. In a physical sense, there was nothing around him, but his senses were heightened beyond anything he had ever tasted, felt, seen, heard, or smelled on earth. This was an absolutely incredible experience! The light had grown to the point where nothing else could be seen or experienced. It had fully surrounded him. He was engulfed in the middle of the light, yet he was still traveling forward. It became brighter and brighter, but instead of blinding him, it invigorated him. But then he remembered he no longer had physical eyes to be blinded, and that he was now a fully spiritual being; the light could not affect something that he no longer possessed.

Suddenly, David saw heaven. It looked like a city, but it was not a city. It looked like a palace, but it was not a palace. It looked like a garden, but it was not a garden. It looked like a mountain, but it was not a mountain. It was breathtaking; it looked like nothing he had ever seen before. No words could describe what he was seeing. There seemed to be physical buildings, but his spirit passed right through them. He could see other spiritual beings all around him now, and everyone was moving in the same direction. Everyone was being drawn toward the most majestic structure of all. It could not be described in human terms, but David knew he was about to enter the throne room of God. The light became brighter, and suddenly he found himself on the threshold of the room. His spirit had stopped. The pull had ceased, and instinctively he knew that he had complete freedom to move about as he wished. He paused a moment, then stepped into the room. Without warning, he was knocked flat. If he had thought that the light had been strong before, it was nothing compared to what it was now. Millions upon millions of times brighter, it saturated anything and everything that entered that room. The power in the throne room was beyond comprehension. It was thick in the air. It was this power that had knocked him to the ground as he entered. He lay prostrate in awe at the glory and majesty that rippled from the huge throne set up in the middle of the room. From a human perspective, David could not help but feel fearful of such might. All around him, the spirits of people were being knocked to the floor as they worshipped.

Here was God, unhidden and revealed in all His glory.

———◈◈◈———

For the first moment, Jason's experience was very similar to David's. He experienced the same "vision" that David experienced. He could see, but it was without the human vision he had been used to. He too was now immortal. All his senses were also increased. He began to feel the same strong pull that David had felt, and he began to move upward.

But these were the only experiences that the two had in common. Jason immediately felt an intense sense of remorse for his last actions while on earth. He had felt guilt before, but nothing like he was experiencing now. He felt a pervading sense of doom and disaster come over his spirit. The pinpoint of light appeared ahead of him, but he could not enjoy it. He could sense dark forms flitting all around him. To one side of the light was a deep gulf. He could feel evil oozing out of it. He began to feel a slight pull toward that darkness as well, but he continued toward the light because that pull was somewhat stronger. He instinctively knew that there was probably no hope for him, and that thought alone made him want to shrivel up into nothing. And to make matters worse, he realized that he had more sensitivity to his emotions and his surroundings than he had ever experienced before. Not only that, but the horrible truth that this would last forever clawed at his already terrified thoughts. As he drew closer to the light, Jason could feel the dark pit trying to tear him away from his trajectory toward the light.

Suddenly, he burst into the light and all other sensations faded away, except for the beautiful glory of his surroundings. He knew he was about to enter heaven. Gone was the resistance that he had felt as he was coming toward the light. Gone was everything but Jason's intense desire to stay right here in this place of perfection forever.

———⇒●⇐———

The puzzle had been solved. Information from eyewitnesses and friends had been pieced together and revealed that Jason's intent had been to shoot and kill Michael. David had seen him raise the gun, tackled Michael to the ground, and in the process inadvertently placed his body in the path of the bullet. The projectile had traveled straight through David's heart, and he died instantly. Michael's head hit the concrete sidewalk, and he was knocked unconscious. Jason, realizing that he had shot the wrong person, had then shot himself.

This information was publicly released on Tuesday morning, the day after the events occurred. Donny sat in his room, red-eyed from lack of sleep and from weeping. He just did not understand. "Why, God?" he asked. "Why?"

His body felt as if it was being torn apart from the grief, frustration, and confusion.

The whole story actually made sense to him, knowing what David had told him about his run-ins with Michael and Jason. Sheer rage flamed up inside of Donny as he thought about Michael's actions. *If Michael hadn't been such a jerk to Jason, none of this would've happened! Michael is the reason my best friend is dead!* Donny's face twisted in a snarl of hate. *It's just not fair that my friend is dead and you're alive, Michael Dervin!* Everything inside him wished that Michael was dead too. He knew this feeling was wrong, but his emotions were currently ruling.

It was then that Donny saw David's journal lying on a stack of books on his desk. He thought about David's abruptness yesterday morning and remembered how out of place it was for David to act like that. He thought it odd that this behavior had come right before David's death. Donny stood and walked over to his roommate's desk. He stared at the journal. David had told him that he would see the journal entry sometime. He hesitated, unsure of whether he should take the liberty of reading his friend's journal at a time like this, but he couldn't imagine a better time.

Slowly, he reached out and touched the worn leather cover. Memories and mental images flooded through Donny as he recalled his friend and all the entries inside this book. Another wave of grief and anger flooded over him, and it seemed as if his body was being pummeled by a thousand tsunamis all at once.

He picked up the journal, and as he did so, two envelopes fell out from between the pages. Donny picked them up and almost fell over when he saw one of them had his name on it. The other had Andrea's name. He ripped open his envelope as fast as he could and impatiently grabbed the folded paper inside. As he unfolded it, his hands began to tremble. It read:

Dear Donny,

Hey bud! I don't know when you'll find this, but I hope it's shortly after I graduate. Yes, I knew I was going to pass on from this life. Don't ask how I knew; Andrea will tell you if you ask her. She will be able to answer your questions after she reads the letter I left for her. Would you please deliver that to her? Leave her alone while she reads it; I'm sure she'll need some space. Afterwards, be there for her as you both deal with this situation. I know this must be terrible for you, but I wanted to leave one last bit of communication with you. Donny, not many people get to do this before they pass on, but I wanted to thank you for everything. You mean so much to me, and you always will. You're like the brother that I never had. Now I'm asking you to do something very important for me. I'm asking you to continue to further the gospel in everything you do. I'm asking you to reach out to people around you every day. And reach out to Michael for me. He's hurting a lot inside and he needs help. Nobody can give him that help except for someone who knows Jesus. You do. Make an impact on his life, Donny. This is all I ask. Oh, one more thing. I give you permission to read my last journal entry now. When you're done, please pass it on to my other friends and family. Thanks, Donny. Words cannot express my appreciation to you. Stay strong and don't grieve. Before you know it, we'll be side-by-side again, lavishing in the awesome presence of God Almighty.

Love from your bro,
David

With tears blurring his vision, Donny reached for the journal and began reading his friend's final testament during his life on earth.

To all my friends and family,

Greetings to my loved ones in the name of the Lord! He is great! My final wish while here on earth is that you would not mourn too much for me. I know mourning is a natural thing; however, I beg you not to draw it out unnecessarily. I am happy, more happy than you could ever know or that I even know as I write this. But trust me. I am so happy, and I don't want you to grieve. God's plan is sovereign. His reign is supreme. Who are we to question His ways?

I don't know how I will pass on from this life to the next, but I have some ideas. For some reason, God has impressed Romans 12:16–21 on my heart .

"Be of the same mind toward one another; do not be haughty in mind, but associate with the lowly. Do not be wise in your own estimation. Never pay back evil for evil to anyone. Respect what is right in the sight of all men. If possible, so far as it depends on you, be at peace with all men. Never take your own revenge, beloved, but leave room for the wrath of God, for it is written, 'Vengeance is Mine, I will repay,' says the Lord. 'But if your enemy is hungry, feed him, and if he is thirsty, give him a drink; for in so doing you will heap burning coals on his head.' Do not be overcome by evil, but overcome evil with good."

Whatever ends up happening to me, I don't want you, my loved ones, to direct anger or wrath towards anyone who might have had a part in it. I don't want you to sin on my behalf. The Scriptures are crystal-clear. It says "never" pay back evil for evil. It says "never" take your own revenge. It also says to be at peace with all men "so far as it depends on you." It depends on you now. For my sake, live in forgiveness. Do not live in bitterness and anger and resentment. Forgive, and be forgiven. The pain of your loss will not disappear; that's not what I'm saying; but you'll handle it a lot better if you let go of the situation and put it in God's hands.

Forgiveness cannot change the past, but it certainly does enlarge the future.

I love each and every one of you. I trust my words will be of some encouragement to you. Live with no regrets. Expend your lives for the gospel. It is a beautiful thing living for the glory of Him who has given us His all. How can we but give Him our all in return?

Love,
David

Donny laid the journal aside, buried his head in his hands, and wept. He wept in grief for the loss of his friend, he wept in repentance for his evil thoughts toward Michael, but most of all he wept tears of thanksgiving to the Lord for giving him the opportunity to know someone as committed to serving God as David Pearl.

14

HEAVEN, HELL, AND SOMEWHERE IN-BETWEEN

Shortly after David fell on his face in the presence of God, he felt himself being raised up again. Still afraid to move, he hesitantly looked up to see an angel supporting him. Although he did look a little intimidating, for some reason David did not fear this heavenly being. It was the power that rippled down from the great throne that commanded all of David's respect.

Suddenly, the angel spoke to him, "Greetings in the name of the Lord! I am Sunar. I have been sent to be your guide. It will soon be time for your meeting."

David found that he could endure the presence of God a lot better when he leaned on Sunar's shoulder. "Meeting? What meeting?"

"Your meeting with the Lord. You must stand before Him in judgment. The judgment is proceeding now. Have you not noticed it?"

David listened for a moment. Suddenly he heard it. It was a voice like none other. It was the voice of God. No human vocal chord could ever have issued the sound that was coming forth from the throne. David hadn't noticed it before, but it was almost as though there were different levels of hearing in heaven. He found he could switch back and forth between them almost like changing channels on a radio station. He had been caught up in the worship of everyone around him when he entered the back of the room, but as he and Sunar slowly made their way forward, David found that he could listen to all "channels" at once. He didn't know how, but he clearly heard God speaking to someone. His voice was indescribable. Then he heard the person speak in answer to a question God had asked her. Instantly, David knew everything about that person's life. It boggled David's mind. He just knew. Everything. All at once. He could see every shameful thing this person had ever committed and every deed worthy of praise. He suddenly realized that this person was standing in judgment before the throne of the living God. He began to feel weak again and leaned heavily on Sunar.

Sunar looked at him. "Do not fear, David. Everyone must be judged, but I can tell you, you have nothing to worry about. I am Sunar. I am in rank just below Michael the Archangel. I have the job of escorting all those saints who have given their life for the cause of the gospel. You have been counted worthy of joining the martyrs' ranks."

David was stunned. "I didn't die because I believed in Jesus. I was just in the wrong place at the wrong time, or should I say, the right place at the right time. But I am not a martyr."

"You did die because you believed in Jesus," Sunar replied. "You were only talking to Michael because you were a follower of Christ. You never would have been hit by that bullet if you had not served Jesus. You did, and you died for it. Do not question what has been commanded by the Father."

David still could not believe that this honor had been bestowed upon him, but he turned his attention to the scene that was being played out at the foot of the throne. He again marveled that he had access to the information about this unknown person who was being judged. Every detail, every action, and every sin in this person's life was made known to everyone in heaven. David could sense the shame and embarrassment of this person, and yet at the same time no one looked down on her because of her actions. If anything, it made everyone more aware of their own shortcomings.

David realized that the current judgment was coming to an end, and he became acutely aware of the fact that there was only one person left before it was his turn. He again turned his attention toward the throne. The Lord was speaking.

"My daughter. You have lived a life pleasing to Me. You have failed on many occasions. You had many opportunities that you missed. But these failures have vanished before Me. They have been washed away by the blood of My beloved son, Jesus. You stand holy and pure before Me, My daughter. Well done, good and faithful servant. You have been faithful with a few things, so I will put you in charge of many things. Enter into the joy of your master!"

Caught up in the moment, David clapped and cheered at the top of his lungs for this sister who had lived a life for the Lord. Her sins were forgotten, and she could look forward to an eternity of joy in the presence of God. Filled with excitement the likes of which David had never seen before, this woman whirled off into the crowd of others who had already made heaven their home.

The next person to stand before the judgment seat was led forward by an angel, and David realized that he was next in line. He began to feel weak again and leaned heavily on Sunar's shoulder. The big angel just smiled and bobbed his head in an encouraging nod.

David's attention returned to the judgment. He could not look directly at the throne because of the incredible light, so he focused on the person who stood before the

Lord. With lowered eyes, the man waited for the Lord to speak.

"Richard Sevening, what did you do with the life that I gave you?" The voice of the Lord came like a wall of water washing over everything and everyone present. As soon as these words were uttered, David immediately had the knowledge of everything that had happened in this man's life. It was all there. Nothing was hidden; all was exposed.

"Lord…Lord, I…I lived a good life. I gave money to the poor. I took care of my children. I never cheated on my wife. I only lied a few times about little things. I'm…"

"Enough!" God's one word crashed around, and Mr. Sevening lowered his head. "If you say you are a good person by pointing out all the *good* things you did in your life, then I would just as easily be able to say you are a bad person by pointing out all the *bad* things you did. Maybe you didn't cheat on your wife, Richard, but judging by the constant thoughts you had about other women, you might as well have performed the action. Have I not said that looking at another woman with lust in your heart is as adultery?"

"I didn't know that, Your Majesty. You cannot judge me against something I didn't know."

"You did not know because you did not want to know, Richard. I sent many people your way to share My Word with you. You brushed them all off. You wanted nothing to do with Me. It is your own fault you did not know. As for the lies, there is no 'little' lie in My eyes. All are equal. They all hurt Me the same. You have failed. But that is not what I hold against you. You rejected My son, My one and only son, Jesus Christ, who died for you. I sent Him for you. You rejected Him, Richard. You mocked Him. You refused to accept His love and His free gift of mercy. You are now a wretched man indeed."

"But, Lord…"

"Not everyone who says to Me, 'Lord, Lord,' will enter the kingdom of heaven, but he who does My will, will enter. I never knew you, Richard Sevening. Depart from Me, you who practice lawlessness!"

Mr. Sevening began to beg for mercy. But as two angels grabbed him and escorted him from the throne, he began to curse God at the top of his lungs. His obscenities suddenly disappeared. David was shaken to his very core. It was indeed a terrible thing to see the wrath of God poured out. David felt about ready to collapse. It was his turn to stand before the throne. Sunar whispered in his ear. "David Pearl, do not fear. It is God's desire never to be angry with anyone. It is every human's choice to accept or reject the love of God. The Lord would be unjust if he did not punish those who disobeyed Him. Do not fear now. You are loved by God. Go now, and go in faith."

Sunar gave David a little push and suddenly he felt much stronger and able to stand and move on his own. Taking a deep breath, he walked out onto the platform. Staring at the ground, he waited.

The muffled beeping sound of a machine broke into the otherwise quiet room. Slowly, corners became pits of darkness as the sun stopped shining through the lone window. A curtain stretched askew across one side of the room. The floor was immaculate; no crumbs or dirt could be seen anywhere, and all surfaces were dust-free. Although occupied, the hospital room was deathly still. A short figure stepped into the room, took a quick look at the prone figure on the bed, and stepped out. It was Tuesday evening, and Michael Dervin was still unconscious. He had been in this state since Monday morning when his head hit the concrete. It was not normal for a patient to remain in this state for so long, and the doctors were worried, but all they could do was wait and watch him.

"Is there any change?"

Doctor Mallory looked up at the nurse that had asked the question as he stepped out of Michael's room. He shook his head. "No, eh, I'm afraid not. I, mmmmm don't understand it, I just don't understand it. Why is he not, um, awake yet…awake yet?"

The nurse only shrugged as the stubby doctor shuffled off muttering to himself.

At the moment, Michael was unable to see, hear, or speak, but he was well aware of himself. He seemed to be in a dark room, and he could sense someone was with him, although he was not afraid. *Am I dead?* he thought. *If I'm dead… then who is with me? And if I'm not, then why is everything so dark? Why can't I feel anything?*

Suddenly, a voice spoke. It was the calmest, richest, most comforting voice he had ever heard. "Michael, you are not dead."

Michael was startled, but it was impossible for him to jump because he could not move. *How…how d-d-d…how did you know that's what I was thinking? And who…who are you?"*

Again came the voice, and again, Michael felt peace wash over him. "I know everything. I know all your thoughts. I am God."

That confused Michael. He had never heard of God talking to someone who was not dead. *Are you sure I'm not dead?*

"Yes."

Then where am I? And why am I here?

"You're here because I needed to tell you that you must go back. I am not finished with you. Your time is not yet up. Now you must go. Go quietly. Go in peace. Sleep, Michael, sleep. And when you awake, you will not remember Me. You will remember none of what took place here. It will be as if you never experienced it. But sleep, my child, sleep.

———➤●◄———

Michael's breathing changed from shallow to normal. Slowly he moved from an unconscious state into a normal, deep, natural sleep, regaining his strength the way God intended humans to do. He slept quietly. He slept in peace. And he slept until the Lord commanded him to awaken.

15

Judgment and Memories

David waited. He could not bring himself to look at the throne. The suspense was incredible, but somehow he managed to continue standing. After what seemed like eternity itself, he heard the voice of the Lord. Each time God spoke, David marveled at how different the voice was. The last time He spoke, it sounded like rushing water. Now it reminded him of the soothing crackling of a campfire.

"David Pearl, what did you do with the life that I gave you?"

David continued staring at the ground. "Lord, I don't know what to say to You. I know I have fallen short many times, but I have tried to live according to Your Word. I have tried to imitate the life of Your Son and share His good news with those around me. I have tried to stay pure before You. I was getting to know Andrea Hutchens very well, but I tried to keep that relationship pure because I didn't want it to get in the way of my relationship with You…"

God interrupted, "Since you brought that up, David, let's talk about that. I want you to think about your relationship with Andi. Do you feel you had an emotional attachment toward her?"

David was silent for a moment before speaking, "Yes, I guess so Lord, but didn't I do all I could to keep our relationship pure?"

"You did very well, my son. I am proud of you for what you did. I know it took determination and discipline. But you must understand that my standard is perfection. Think back to all those times that in your mind you saw yourself as already being married to her. Did you ever think about taking a break from the relationship and cutting down on the time you spent with her so that you could refocus all of your energy and life on Me? You could have done better, David. However, I want you to know that I am very well pleased with all the steps you took to keep that relationship pure. You did well."

David was still looking downward, but inside he felt joy flow through him at the sound of His Master's praise. However, any bubble of excitement that he had was suddenly burst as the Lord continued.

"David, how do you feel you used the resources that I gave you?"

David knew instantly what He was talking about. Before David's radical experience with the Lord, he had not been the most generous person on the face of the earth. Often he had wasted his money on things that were not needed, and many of them just collected dust. "Your Majesty, I tithed ten percent of everything I earned."

"David, did you think that ten percent was a number that I pulled out of the air and that if I received that I would be happy? If so, you were mistaken. You know My Scripture says that I do not care about the sacrifices and rituals of My people as much as I care about their hearts. I do not care about numbers. I care about hearts. I want to see hearts that are willing to give and to trust Me with everything. If you can surrender your money and material goods to Me, then I can trust you with much more."

David stood there in shame, knowing that he had caused His Savior and Father sorrow. "I'm sorry, Lord. I wish I had it to do over again, but I cannot. I lived my life once, and now it is done. All I can say is that I am sorry and ask for Your forgiveness, my Lord."

There was a short silence, and then a sound like laughter. With the gravity of the moment, this act of amusement from God surprised him. Why would God laugh when he asked for forgiveness?

"Oh, David. Have you ever tried speaking with someone who will not look you in the eye?" The Lord laughed again. "David Pearl, the one with living eyes, the one who did not fear to look anyone in the eye. I want you to look at Me now."

David's head was still bowed. He closed his eyes. He honestly felt fear at the thought of looking at God. He could barely make himself do it, but with eyes still closed, he raised his head toward the throne. He paused.

The Lord's voice came in a barely audible whisper. "Open your eyes, my son."

David's eyes flashed open. Unable to move a muscle, David stood transfixed and feasted his eyes on God—the Creator, Father, Lord, and Savior of the entire earth. No longer were his eyes blinded by the brilliance of the Lord. He could now miraculously bear the light. God could never be described in words. All David could do was stand and stare, lost in the mystery and awesomeness of God.

The low laughter came again. "That's better." Then He grew serious. "David, you have already been forgiven. Yes, you have fallen short in many areas. But it does not matter because you trusted in my Son, Jesus, to deal with your shortcomings. His blood has washed away your sins, and you stand before Me pure and without blemish. I take joy in looking at you even more than you do in looking at Me. You are holy. You are righteous. You are my son, and I love you. Well done, good and faithful servant. You have been faithful with a few things, so I will put you in charge of many things. Enter into the joy of your Master!"

Wednesday morning dawned bright and sunny. The air was still crisp from the evening chill, but spring flowers were opening up everywhere for a new day. The sunny atmosphere, however, did not mirror the emotions within Andrea's heart. She lay in bed without moving. Last night had been a late night. She had not been able to fall asleep for a long time; the anvil of sorrow that she felt inside weighed heavily on her mind for hours. Looking over at her clock, she realized that she had slept in; it was ten o'clock. It didn't matter of course, since classes had been canceled for the rest of the week due to the tragedy.

Andrea lay with her eyes shut, never wanting to open them again. Reality was too bitter. She had cried so much the past few days that she did not understand how she could continue to shed tears, but still they came. Even now, a drop squeezed from under her right eyelid and slid down the side of her face onto the pillow. She brushed away the trail left by the tear as her mind turned again to her friend and the good times she had experienced with him.

She remembered the night that she had driven to David's church for the healing service. She remembered seeing him at the front of the altar in his wheelchair and feeling so sorry for him, and yet thankful that he was not hurt worse. She remembered asking him what would have happened if something worse had occurred and she had lost him. With the pain of his loss so fresh in her mind, she could recall vividly every word that he had said: "I didn't die. But someday I will, so don't upset yourself too much when it happens. Just remember that when it happens, I'm at home with my Savior!"

She gasped as the enormity of his words struck home. Those words had been spoken for this very moment. Her mind wandered on to the night of her birthday, when she learned that David had been healed. Again, she recalled his words, and again, they spoke to her heart: "Life is not always going to be bright and shining as it is now. You will not see miracles happen in every circumstance. There will be times when it seems that God is very distant and unresponsive to things happening in your life. There will be times when life is just the opposite of tonight, times when you have no reason to celebrate. But remember what this joy feels like, keep it close to you. We are to rejoice always, in everything. Stay joyful, Andrea!"

Thought after thought swirled around Andrea. Memory after memory flooded through her. Next, she remembered the conversation she had had with David just one short week ago when she told him about her dream. She had asked him what he thought it meant. His reply came to her almost word for word. "I have no clue, Andi. All I know is that God wants you to remember the joy you felt when you stood in His presence. Remember that when you hit the tidal waves of hardship that will certainly come. I don't know what your dream is supposed to mean, but you'll understand it when the time is right. He wanted you to have that experience for a reason, and He'll show you what it means."

Andrea rolled over, cradled her face in her hands, and wept as David's voice came to her one final time. "Andi, no matter what happens in life, I want you to promise me several things. I want you to promise me that you'll always trust in God. I want you to promise that you'll always remember that no matter what happens in life, He is still in control, He still loves you, and He still has a perfect plan that cannot be hindered by anything. I want you to promise that you'll expend your life for the gospel and that you'll press on and live for Jesus no matter what happens to discourage you or tear you down. I want you to promise me these things." Andrea's mind went blank for a moment. Then swirling, bouncing, reverberating, two words burst through her mind, and she heard her own voice repeating over and over, "I promise, I promise, I *promise!*"

A fresh batch of tears came to her eyes as Andrea realized that somehow she had to pull through this and live up to her promises. *Why? Why did he have to make me promise those things?*

Just then, a knock sounded on her door. She ignored it. She did not want to see anybody. Not only was she not in the mood for company, but she was definitely not presentable with her snarled hair, tear-stained face, and pajamas. The visitor, however, was not to be ignored, and after listening to a full minute of knocking, Andrea got up and looked through the peephole. It was Donny.

Andrea sighed, wiped at her eyes, and opened the door. Donny looked up. "I'm sorry to bother you, Andrea. I know how you're feeling and I won't keep you long, but I needed to give you something. I couldn't wait any longer." Andrea noticed for the first time that an envelope was tucked under Donny's arm. He handed it to her and her heart flipped as she immediately recognized the handwriting.

Barely able to speak, she whispered, "What is this?"

"I found this in David's journal. He asked me to give it to you. He also left one for me." Just the thought of his friend's letter was such a reminder of his loss that pain shot through Donny's body. They stood looking at each other for a moment, Donny struggling with his thoughts and Andrea almost in shock. Then Donny turned and slowly walked away.

Andrea could not think clearly. She heard Donny leave, but the thought never occurred to her to say good-bye. She walked back into her room, closed the door, and sat down on her bed. Her mind was in a daze. Her fingers traced over the name scrawled on the envelope. She could almost see him sitting at his desk, writing that name. Her name. She did not seem to be able to open the envelope. Her brain kept giving the signal, but her hands were unwilling. She was almost scared to read what was inside.

Finally, with tensed nerves, her trembling fingers began ripping at the seal. Inside was a piece of notebook paper neatly folded into thirds. With her heart thudding, Andrea slowly opened it to see the careful lines of David's handwriting.

Dear Andi,

How I wish I could find the right words. What do you say at a time like this? I really don't know, so I will just start writing. I am about to pass on from this life. I really don't know why I just said that because, obviously, you know that if you're reading this right now. I can't seem to get the right tense here. You have no idea how weird it is trying to write a note that will be read after you're gone.

Anyhow, I need to explain something to you. Do you remember when we were talking on the dock at Spring Retreat? Do you remember how beautiful it was? Do you remember the sun and the lake? Do you remember the flowers? Do you remember how peaceful I was? Do you remember how I suddenly lost that peace all in one moment? I have never had such a premonition as I did at that moment. I don't know if you remember, but a dark cloud slid across the sun. In that instant, God showed me what your dream meant. He showed me that I was the one you saw dancing before His throne. He showed me that I was about to graduate from this life. I apologize for scaring you like I did, but you have no idea what it is like to see yourself dead. Even now I feel as if my body is about to explode into a thousand tiny pieces. But it is okay, because at the same time I can feel God inside me, giving me strength. He will enable me to get through, and He will enable you to get through as well. Please do not grieve too long. Let it out, but then move on. For my sake, Andi, move on.

Andrea, how I wish I could have served God with you for many more years. Yet I understand that this is God's perfect plan and that I must go. But I want to remind you of the promises you made that morning on the dock. You promised me that you would serve God with everything you have. You also promised that you would rest in the fact that God is fully in control, even when things seem like they are out of control, probably like they do now. Allow His arms to wrap you in His loving embrace. I am about to see Him face to face, and before you know it, you will too. Death comes faster than anyone can imagine. Live each day as if it is your last, because one day it will be. Do everything in your power to spread the love of Jesus to those around you. Build up the believers, raise up the lost, and never take your eyes off Jesus. He alone is worthy. Do not hold bitterness in your heart. Do not hang on to your grief, let it run its course, but do not wallow in it. It will paralyze you, and that is just what Satan wants. Do not worry about me, or your friends, or earthly things, but put Him first and He will supply all your needs, including your need for love.

Thank you so much for your friendship and your faithfulness. Thank you for your example. Thank you for the memories and the laughs. Thank you for everything. Now dry your tears. Look up for salvation draweth nigh! The Lord is coming soon! Live for Him and be prepared for His coming! Amen.

16

A Death and a Birth

Jason's spirit was deposited just outside the throne room of God Almighty. He instantly discovered that he was capable of moving under his own power. With a shout, he reveled in the freedom he was now experiencing. On earth he never had the joy of walking on his own; now, however, he could move around as he pleased. But even with this newfound liberty, Jason was not as quick to step inside the throne room. Taking his time, he turned and paused to take in the full glowing picture that lay before him. The sun did not exist, yet everything was bathed in the brightest, clearest light Jason had ever beheld. Suddenly, he realized that the source of this light streamed from behind him. He turned around again and stepped hesitantly into the throne room of the great I Am.

Instantly, he was knocked to the floor. He had been blown away by the grandeur and splendor of everything he had seen up until now, but none of that could compare to the feeling of majesty that rippled in thick waves throughout the room. If Jason had to breathe like he did back on earth, he would have been gasping for breath in awe and fear. Terror-stricken, he tried to run away. He knew that he was now powerless to stand up, but he tried to wriggle backward out of the room. To his dismay, he found that he was even incapable of this small movement.

Without warning, Jason was hoisted to his feet and marched toward the middle of the room. A stone-faced angel walked beside him, practically carrying him along. Jason tried to resist, but the angel was too strong. Finally they stopped, and Jason saw that he was in a short line of others who were waiting for judgment. Jason began to hear the conversation at the foot of the throne, which he tried to block out. His mind was way too busy trying to figure out what he would say to God when it was his turn.

Consumed with his fear, Jason was oblivious to the fact that his dread came from the existence of sin in his life that was not forgiven. Now it was revealed and exposed to the presence of a perfect, holy God. God cannot tolerate sin; it must be dealt with. Because of his sin, Jason could not enjoy the love and mercy of the most amazing One in the universe.

Instead, the war inside him raged on. He tried again to wrench himself from the grasp of the big angel. With every spiritual muscle in his new spiritual body, he fought this supernatural being. The angel, however, had no problem restraining him. For the first time, the angel spoke. "Be still.

It is over, Jason. You lived your life once, and now it is done. What is done is done, and you can't go back. Now you must answer for what you have done with your life."

Jason fell limp in the angel's grasp and gave in to his fate before the throne of God. He remembered David warning him that he only had one life to find God. It had all made sense to him then, but he never thought the end of his life would come so quickly. He tried to forget the rest of David's words, hoping that they were all false. With each moment, his fear grew. He pinched himself, hoping that this was all a vivid dream and that it would end at any moment. Another wave of panic washed over him as he realized that what he was experiencing was real. *How could this be?* he thought. *This isn't supposed to be happening! Why was I so stupid? There has to be a way out of this! Everything I've heard about God says that He is loving. He wouldn't send someone like me who has been downcast, made fun of, and paralyzed my whole life to a place like hell!* Jason tried to quell his fear, but it kept rising.

Absorbed in his thoughts, Jason hadn't noticed the line in front of him dwindling. In horror, he felt himself being pushed out of the crowd. He heard his accompanying angel saying, "It is your turn, Jason. You must face the consequences of your actions. Go now."

Out of options, Jason shuffled slowly toward the throne. With his head down and eyes tightly shut, he waited; his terror building to an indescribable height. He still did not know why he felt such fear. But it was there, and it forced him to his knees. Jason could feel the power that was directed toward him from the throne, and he felt as if he should be burning to a crisp beneath its force.

Like a descending axe, the Lord's voice cut through his thoughts. "Jason Portello, what did you do with the life that I gave you?"

Jason paused. He could not seem to be able to find his voice. Finally, he stuttered, "I…I…I did what I could." He paused. When he heard what he had said, he thought it sounded pretty lame, so he continued, "Up until the end of my life, I didn't do anything *really* bad. I was the one that everybody else picked on all the time. Why are you punishing me instead of them? I understand that murder is wrong, but I was driven to it by others. Don't you know that?"

God answered with what sounded like sorrow in his voice, "Jason, I do not approve of what so many people did to you. They mistreated you and therefore will receive the full recompense of their deeds. But, Jason, this is not about them. This judgment is about you. And you seem to be mistaken. I am not judging you on your actions. I am judging you on your acceptance or rejection of My Son, Jesus Christ. Your name is not found in the Lamb's book of life."

Trying to hide his fear and hoping desperately to prolong the inevitable, Jason spoke, "Lord, that seems a bit unfair to me. You never showed Yourself to me. You never even spoke to me. This doesn't seem to be very fair."

The Lord waited. "Do you have any other complaints before I answer you, Jason?" Jason's head drooped further. He did not, and both of them knew it. "This trial is more than fair, Jason. I did show Myself to you. I did speak to you. I spoke to you through the voice and body of David Pearl. He was just one of the many servants that I use mightily every day to reveal Myself to others. The words he spoke to you were given to him by Me. The actions he showed you were nothing but pure love. I care for you, and so did David. I love you, Jason. That is why I must judge you and punish you."

Once again, Jason found the courage to interject, "Lord, it does not seem very loving to send someone you love into eternal fire and torment."

"I love everyone, Jason. I even love Michael Dervin, who tried to make your life as miserable as possible. I love everyone regardless of what they have done, and I desire them to come to Me. That is why I sent Jesus to earth, to show My love. Because I love you all, I must give you a choice. Otherwise, everyone would be forced to love Me. I give everyone created in My image the choice to accept My gift of love, or to reject it. You rejected Me and therefore must accept the consequences. But just because you did not love Me does not mean that I do not love you. I love you dearly, and it sorrows Me to see this happen. You stand guilty before Me, Jason. Your sin is revealed before Me, unhidden and uncovered. The only way that anyone can join Me in eternity is to accept the sacrifice of My Son, Jesus. You never did that. I never knew you, Jason Portello. Depart from Me, you who practice lawlessness!"

With those words, Jason's deepest fears had been confirmed. A sinister spirit that had never revealed itself before began to rise up in Jason, and he began cursing the Lord unmercifully. His words of hate did not last long, however, as he felt himself forcefully shoved from the room. His rage blinded him, and he suddenly felt himself on the edge of what he knew to be a deep precipice. His rage gave way to terror, and he frantically fought the vice-like grip of his guardian, but nothing could help him now. A wicked stench rose to him from the pit, and he could feel an immeasurable heat rising from below. He didn't know how he felt the heat because there was nothing physical about him, but it was very real and very painful—more painful than anything Jason had ever experienced on earth. He screamed, begging his captor not to throw him in, but even as he screamed, he felt himself being thrown over the edge.

Eternity had begun.

Donny's nose wrinkled in distaste as he entered the Pinevale Regional Hospital. He hated hospitals. The smell itself was enough to make him sick, let alone all the germs and bugs lurking in the corners. This time was even worse as there was an intense emotional battle waging inside him.

Here he was, in an elevator that was taking him to see the very person who was at the center of his current heartache. Everything inside of him was screaming at him to turn around and leave. And yet, with a set jaw and a resolute heart strengthened by his friend's last words, he stepped off on the eighth floor and located room 823.

Praying constantly, he paused to take a quick breath and collect his thoughts. Then he stepped around the doorframe and into the room. A nurse stood by the bed talking with Michael. "We really don't know what happened to you," she was saying. "You were unconscious for so long that you're really not supposed to be alive. All our tests show that you're in good shape except for that bump on your head. You're just weak and tired. We will be sending you home tonight. So rest up! Oh…" the nurse had turned abruptly to face Donny. "I didn't see you there! Are you here to see Michael?"

Donny nodded, "Yes, ma'am."

"Okay, I'll leave you two alone. Just take it easy, Michael! Remember, you're supposed to be building your strength. I'll be back in to check on you later." And with that, she whipped around the door and disappeared.

Donny sighed, walked slowly over to the bedside and sat down. "Hello, Michael."

Michael had been looking at him very curiously. With a confused look, he asked, "Who are you? I don't know you, do I?"

Donny shook his head. "My name is Donny. No, you don't know me. But you know someone that I do. Or should I say *did*." He paused as he scrutinized Michael's face. "David Pearl was my best friend."

Michael's expression changed from a look of curiosity to one of fear. He shrank to the other side of the bed. "You're here for some sort of revenge, aren't you?" His voice quavered in fear.

Donny's eyebrow went up. That wasn't exactly the response he was expecting. Quickly, he reassured him. "No, Michael, that's not why I'm here." Michael's relief was visible, but his suspicion lingered, so Donny added, "Relax, you don't need to worry. I'm not here to hurt you."

"Okay, then why are you here?"

Donny closed his eyes for a brief moment and sighed, asking God for strength. "Michael, I'm here to tell you that...that God loves you." He watched Michael's face to catch the response.

At first Michael didn't know what to think. His first thought was to get angry, but after noticing the bags under Donny's red eyes, he realized that he bore no malice toward him for David's death. Here was someone who had every right to be livid with him for causing the death of his best friend, someone who had no reason to love him, and yet... he did. He had said the exact same thing that David had said every time they parted ways. Goose bumps covered Michael's flesh, and he began to feel something that he had never felt before. This was love. He raised his eyebrows inquisitively and whispered, "Why? Just why? Why do you come here and tell me this? Shouldn't you be mad at me?"

Donny smiled. "Why? Because I care for you just like David did. You're dying, Michael. And when I say dying, I don't mean physically, I mean spiritually. You're missing the one thing in your life that really makes life worth living. You're on a fast track that's headed straight to hell, and it's only by the grace of God that you're not there right now. You have sinned throughout your entire life, and those sins have never been forgiven. When that's the case, you are condemned to hell when you die." Donny saw Michael about to speak, so he held up his finger and kept talking. "But listen to me, Michael. God has given you a second chance. He gave you a second chance on Monday when he spared *your* life by taking David's. And He gave you a second chance thousands of years ago when He sent His Son, Jesus Christ, to die on the cross. You see, Jesus died to take your sins away. The blood He shed on the cross atoned for your sins. But you have to accept that, Michael. You have to believe that He loves you and that He wants you to know Him! You have to chase after Him like He's chased after you! He loves you, Michael!"

Michael cut in, "But why? Why would anyone die for me?"

Donny stared at the floor. Softly, he said, "David did." He paused, then continued, becoming stronger. "You see, the Christian life is all about becoming more like Christ. David was constantly pursuing that, and in his death he became the closest to being like Christ that any human being can get. He died *for* someone else! You see, David embodied the very love of Christ toward you in that he died for you, just like Jesus did! That bullet was meant for you, but David took it to give you a second chance. Now I'm here to tell you that your life, and David's life, will be wasted if you do not find Christ. He is reaching out to you, Michael. He loves you dearly. All you have to do is accept it."

Donny stopped. Tears were running down both of Michael's cheeks, and he was doing nothing to stop them. Donny's words had been hitting home. They were making sense, and Michael finally understood this love. His heart almost burst with remorse for causing David's death and the pain that he had caused so many people. Finally, he whispered, "How, Donny? How do I accept God's love for me? How do I do it?"

Donny smiled. "Just surrender to Him. Tell Him you're ready to accept His love and in response you're going to commit your life to Him no matter what." He closed his eyes as Michael began to pray.

"Oh, God! I barely know what to say to You right now. I guess...I guess I just feel so unworthy! You have shown me my sin! And..." Michael broke down sobbing again. Donny waited patiently and a few minutes later, he managed to continue, "I'm sorry, Jesus. I'm sorry for mocking You. I'm sorry for how I've treated You and Your followers. I'm sorry that I've created this mess. Please forgive me! Please help me to change. Oh God, help me to change! Please take over my life."

A few seconds later, Donny looked up with tears in his own eyes. "Michael," he whispered, "David is smiling right now. I know it. Everything in your past is gone, friend! You get to start living for Jesus today! I'm so excited for you!"

Michael could barely speak. His eyes were blurred with his tears, but he managed to blurt out, "Thank you, Donny. Thank you so much! I feel so clean and free! Thank you! We must get together. I want to know more about God. Look me up, back at school!"

Donny got up to go. "Okay, I will. We will definitely get together. Now get your rest, Michael. You'll need it to get rid of that bump on your head." He walked out with a smile on his face. His heart was just about ready to burst. There was no feeling like leading someone to the fullness of joy found in Christ!

Just as Donny got in the elevator, the nurse rushed down the hall and entered Michael's room. "Michael!" she began. Then she saw his tears. "Are you all right? Is everything okay? Are you in pain?"

Michael managed a grin. "No, I'm fine. Everything is great. These are tears of joy!"

The nurse cocked her head and looked at him sideways. "Well, if you're sure. Here, you got mail. She laid several cards on his lap and left the room.

Michael opened them one by one. They were all get-well cards, most of them sent by family members. Then he came to the last one; he did not recognize the handwriting. He opened it up and skipped all the writing to see who had signed it. It was signed at the bottom in neat little handwriting: Andrea Hutchens.

He had been forgiven.

17

Once and Done

David was lost—utterly, helplessly lost in the grandeur and prestige of the Lord God Almighty. From the moment he had heard the words "Well done, good and faithful servant!" he had been completely absorbed in worshipping the King. The feeling of gratitude that flowed out of him for the sacrifice the Father and Son had made for him was immense. He felt so insignificant and yet…so loved. He had moved around a bit to get used to his new spiritual body and explore some of his surroundings. He had even held some conversations with heroes from the Bible, like David, Noah, Philip, Stephen, and Paul. While on earth, David had always wanted to ask these men questions about their lives. But when he met them, he was struck with how normal they actually were. Besides, their conversations never lasted long anyway because somehow they always got distracted and started worshipping the Lord again. That seemed to be the only thing that mattered.

David turned and found himself face to face with none other than Michael Dervin. David's eyes widened. "Michael! How did you get here so fast?"

Michael laughed "Uh, a car accident, I think? But it doesn't matter. I'm here! Thank you *so* much, David! Your death saved my life!"

David laughed out loud. "Then it was worth it!"

Michael nodded. "Donny led me to Jesus because of what you did for me. But guess what else? You know those college buddies of mine that I used to hang out with? Well, I was able to lead them to Christ before I died! And it was all because of your sacrifice, David! I can never thank you enough. I just stood before the Lord of all creation and He found me *innocent* because Jesus's blood covered all my sins!"

David grinned at Michael's excitement, but couldn't hold it in. He started laughing from sheer joy. Michael joined in until David shouted, "Come on, Michael! Let's go praise the One who loved us and gave everything for us. I've had time to worship Him, but there's something else that I need to do. I want to dance before my Lord and my love. I want to give Him my all. Let's go!"

———⟫●⟪———

Silence reigned supreme in the cozy little house on the corner. An elderly, white-haired lady lay resting beneath the cover of her thick comforter. She was a healthy, spry little woman for her age, but she was tired after a long day of cooking at the local soup kitchen. This day also marked a very important milestone for her. Just hours earlier, she had put the finishing touches to a biography she had been writing about someone that she had known a long time ago. Tomorrow she would send it to the publisher.

Now, she closed her eyelids as sleep began to follow her like her shadow. Lost in her dreams, she suddenly became aware that this dream was exactly the same as one she had a long time ago. She felt herself rising from the earth. Higher and higher she ascended until she felt another surface beneath her feet. All was dark except for one tiny pinpoint of light in the distance. Then someone took her hand. It was the same Person who took her hand when she had this same dream years ago. It was all so real that she could not believe this was a dream. Suddenly, it hit her. This was no dream. This was actually happening. Her Companion began walking her toward the light, which streamed like a river from behind a corner. Ordinarily, the light would have blinded her, but remarkably, she was drawn to it instead. When they reached the corner, she stopped abruptly. She knew for certain that the Lord of hosts was just around the corner and that if she moved beyond the corner, she would die. Her Companion nudged her forward and in a rich, low voice said, "Do not fear, Andrea. Go now...you have been called."

Andrea took a deep breath and took a step into the light. By some miracle, her eyes were able to handle the light, and she could see that it was shining from the most beautiful throne that could be imagined. In that moment, she collapsed in a heap as if dead under the glorious majesty of God. Her Companion, however, raised her up, and Andrea felt new strength course through her body. Quietly, He said, "Look again, Andrea."

She raised her head and saw at the foot of the throne a man. He was dancing with all the strength in his body. His face was obscured to her, but it didn't matter. This time she knew who it was even though she couldn't see his face. Andrea could feel the joy flowing out of this dancer, and all she wanted to do was to run and dance with him before the King of kings and Lord of lords. Without another thought, she gave into the urge and took off as fast as she could. This time her Companion did not restrain her, but His face broadened into a huge smile. With renewed strength, Andrea threw herself into the throng of people and began dancing like she had never danced before. Everything was forgotten. All she wanted was to let it all out before her God. Finally she found herself on the edge of the crowd that stood, danced, and knelt before the throne. She looked around her. Off to one side, she spotted him. With a grin of inexplicable joy, she walked up behind David and tapped him on the shoulder. David spun around and, with a face of confused emotions, exclaimed, "Andrea! How did *you* get here so fast?"

"So fast? I didn't. I lived to be eighty-nine years old!"

"What! Oh! Yes, I keep forgetting that there is no such thing as time up here. It seems like I've been here only a few...a few..."

"A few what?"

David shrugged. "I don't know! I can't remember that word we used to use to measure time. Oh well. The point is, *I* just got here!"

Andrea smiled. "Thank you so much for what you did when we were friends. Not only did you protect your heart, but you allowed me to save mine for my wonderful husband of sixty years! It apparently wasn't for you, and you handled it as such. You have no idea how thankful I am for that."

David frowned as he remembered the Lord's reprimand. He replied, "Sorry I didn't do better. But I tried…and you're welcome."

Suddenly, their conversation was cut short as something slammed into David from one side. Instead of feeling pain and getting thrown to the ground as he would have in his previous life, David was pushed gently sideways and just seemed to float in midair with no injuries. The object, which turned out to be Donny Fresnett, just bounced backward in the same manner. He stood up, laughing long and loud. "Hey, boulderbottom! What've you been up to?"

David grinned back. "Boulderbottom yourself, beetlebrain!"

Just then, Sunar walked by. He raised his eyebrow and looked at David. "Did I just hear you call Donny beetlebrain?"

David slowly shook his head in the most innocent gesture he could think of.

"Good, I don't want to hear either of you two twiddleheads call anybody names!" He walked away with a mischievous smile on his face while the three friends burst into laughter.

David began running. "Come on, you two! Let's worship!"

After what seemed like thirty minutes (but measured in earth time would have been thirty thousand years), David stood before the throne of God. He was staring up into the Lord's face as lost then as he was the first time he had experienced God's beauty and mystery. Finally, he found his voice enough to whisper, "Thank you. Thank you so much! I wish I could say more! But that's it. Thank you, Father."

The Lord smiled. "You're welcome, my son. It was all possible because of the sacrifice of my Son, Jesus. *He died once, and it was done.*"

One thing I have asked from the
Lord, that I shall seek:
That I may dwell in the house of the
Lord all the days of my life,
To behold the beauty of the Lord
And to meditate in His temple.

~ Psalm 27:4 ~

Disclaimer

I recognize that the depiction of life after death in this book is not an exact portrayal of what is described to us in Scripture. I understand that there are different denominational interpretations of the afterlife and that no one will ever know for sure what heaven will be like until we experience it for ourselves.

I understand that the Bible describes several different judgments occurring in the afterlife, mainly the judgment seat (Greek: *bema*) of Christ found in 2 Corinthians 5:10, and the great white throne judgment found in Revelation 20:11–15. I disregarded the individuality of these two events and merged them into one in order to better establish my point.

I acknowledge having taken artistic license in order to illustrate that final day when *every individual* will be judged for deeds done in the body. The scenes of judgment in this book are not meant to *accurately* depict the great day of judgment for Christians or non-Christians, but are for the sole purpose of demonstrating that everyone on earth who is made in God's image will one day be called to give an account to Him for the way in which we lived our lives.

The Bible clearly says that one day we will all face our Maker. In this life, we are only given one chance. Once we have lived our life, it is done. It will be too late to change even one misspoken word! If you have not already done so, please do not wait any longer to get your life right with God. Turn from your sins, and admit to God your need for His help in your life. Make Him the Lord of your life, and trust in Christ to be your Savior. Regardless of whether you are a Christian or a non-Christian, we all need to examine ourselves to determine if we are right with God (2 Corinthians 13:5). Let's live our lives in a manner worthy of Jesus Christ (Colossians 1:10)!

—Jeff Eshenour